MW01153573

Lost Souls

Mending Magic Series, Volume 1

W.J. May

Published by Dark Shadow Publishing, 2018.

This is a work of fiction. Similarities to real people, places, or events are entirely coincidental.

LOST SOULS

First edition. November 22, 2018.

Copyright © 2018 W.J. May.

Written by W.J. May.

Also by W.J. May

Hidden Secrets Saga
Seventh Mark - Part 1
Seventh Mark - Part 2
Marked By Destiny
Compelled
Fate's Intervention
Chosen Three
The Hidden Secrets Saga: The Complete Series

Kerrigan Chronicles
Stopping Time
A Passage of Time
Ticking Clock
Secrets in Time
Time in the City
Ultimate Future

Mending Magic Series
Lost Souls
Illusion of Power
Challenging the Dark
Castle of Power
Limits of Magic

Omega Queen Series
Discipline

The Chronicles of Kerrigan: Gabriel
Living in the Past
Present For Today
Staring at the Future

The Chronicles of Kerrigan Prequel
Christmas Before the Magic
Question the Darkness
Into the Darkness
Fight the Darkness
Alone in the Darkness
Lost in Darkness
The Chronicles of Kerrigan Prequel Series Books #1-3

The Chronicles of Kerrigan Sequel
A Matter of Time
Time Piece
Second Chance
Glitch in Time
Our Time
Precious Time

The Hidden Secrets Saga
Seventh Mark (part 1 & 2)

Shadow of Doubt - Part 1
Shadow of Doubt - Part 2
Four and a Half Shades of Fantasy
Dream Fighter
What Creeps in the Night
Forest of the Forbidden
Arcane Forest: A Fantasy Anthology
The First Fantasy Box Set

Watch for more at www.wjmaybooks.com.

LOST SOULS

MENDING MAGIC SERIES #1

USA TODAY BESTSELLING AUTHOR

W.J. MAY

Copyright 2018 by W.J. May

LOST SOULS

MENDING MAGIC SERIES #1

USA TODAY BESTSELLING AUTHOR

W.J. MAY

Have You Read the C.o.K Series?

The Chronicles of Kerrigan
Book I - *Rae of Hope* is FREE!

BOOK TRAILER:

http://www.youtube.com/watch?v=gILAwXxx8MU

How hard do you have to shake the family tree to find the truth about the past?

Fifteen-year-old Rae Kerrigan never really knew her family's history. Her mother and father died when she was young, and it's only when she accepts a scholarship to the prestigious Guilder Boarding School in England that a mysterious family secret is revealed.

Will the sins of the father be the sins of the daughter?

As Rae struggles with new friends, a new school, and a star-struck forbidden love, she must also face the ultimate challenge: receive a tattoo on her sixteenth birthday with specific powers that may bind her to an unspeakable darkness. It's up to Rae to undo the dark evil in her family's past and have a ray of hope for her future.

Find W.J. May

Website:
http://www.wjmaybooks.com
Facebook:
https://www.facebook.com/pages/Author-WJ-May-FAN-PAGE/
141170442608149
Newsletter:
SIGN UP FOR W.J. May's Newsletter to find out about new releases, updates, cover reveals and even freebies!
http://eepurl.com/97aYf

Mending Magic Series

Lost Souls
Illusion of Power
Challenging the Dark
Castle of Power
Limits of Magic
Protectors of Light

Lost Souls Blurb:

Your curse is your biggest strength.
I just didn't know it yet.

Jamie Hunt's the high school quarterback in his senior year. He's popular, smart, and has the prettiest girl in the school chasing him. Life couldn't be more perfect.

But a single mistake changes everything. His new "ability" puts him in the middle of a war he doesn't want to be a part of, protecting a girl he barely knows, and running from the one thing he loves—his family.

Never give up. Never give in.

Chapter 1

The first time it happened I was five. At least, that's the first time I remember it happening. They say it can start even earlier than that.

My dad and I were at the park, playing baseball. Rather, my dad was on the phone and I was throwing the ball up and catching it by myself. Must have looked kind of pathetic from the outside, but I didn't mind. I was just happy he was spending time with me.

Anyway, the park by our house had this huge fountain. It was a gaudy monstrosity with steps of tiered cement stretching fifty feet into the sky. It had been a community project. One of those, 'let's throw money into an already affluent neighborhood as an excuse to get together for bourbon and cigars and pat ourselves on the back for a job well done'. The fountain was an eyesore, but it was fun in the summer when the weather was hot. It was one of those marble designs with men in military uniform lifting a rock and a few ridiculous cherubs added to make it child-like.

I wandered off a little ways from my dad. Throwing the ball higher and higher, trying to tune out that he was screaming at someone in Japanese. Eventually, I ended up right in front of that fountain. I gave the ball another hard throw, frustrated to have no one to throw it to. Freakin' thing landed right on the top of the fountain. On top of the bloomin' rock the marble men were lifting.

At this point, five-year-old me was in a tough spot. It was a rare occasion that my dad would take me anywhere just for fun, and I did NOT want to screw it all up by losing the ball my uncle had given me. I tried to climb the first few steps, but slipped and fell. I looked for something I could use as a ladder, but there was nothing but grass and perfectly pruned trees as far as the eye could see.

I turned and glared at the ball. Stupid thing.

That's when it happened. Born from that ironic need not to disappoint my father.

One second I was staring up at the fountain. The next, I was sitting at the very top of the rock, those military marble men holding the boulder and me while water cascaded down around them. The baseball held tightly in my hands. A huge grin stretched across my face.

I remember my dad running over. Dropping the phone and shouting. He kept looking over his shoulder like he was terrified someone might see. I didn't realize until much later he was crying. And the shouting—I'd never heard anything like it.

He kept saying, "You climbed up there. You climbed up there all by yourself. You climbed up there. Remember? You CLIMBED up there."

Of course, I had no idea what was happening. I was just happy I'd recovered the ball. A week later, a construction crew tore down that fountain. My dad said it was unrelated. I watched from my bedroom window.

I'd forgotten most of the incident for, like, a decade.

But it's one of my first memories, my dad shouting like that.

It was just a small preview of things to come...

"JAMES!"

My eyes opened slowly, then my heartbeat quickened and I shot up into a sitting position. One hand flew out to silence my alarm before I realized it was my dad yelling from downstairs and not the annoying blaring from my alarm.

"James, get your ass out of bed! You're going to be late for school!"

I pressed a pillow over my face with a silent groan, cursing the sun and all its Southern California consistency. Cursing the addictive video game that had kept me awake until just a few hours before. My feet hit the floor, and I answered before he could call again.

"I'm coming! Gimme two minutes!"

The routine was simple. Brush the teeth. Wash the face. Give up on the hair. Lucinda, our housekeeper, had come by yesterday afternoon and had left a stack of clean clothes on top of my dresser. I threw on the first thing in the pile and made it downstairs with thirty seconds to spare.

My dad was pacing back and forth in the kitchen. It was only seven-thirty, but already a phone was glued to each hand. He lowered them slightly and gestured at a bowl of fruit. "Finally. Get yourself some breakfast—you need to eat something before we head out."

I headed automatically to the cabinet and pulled out a mug. It was just as automatically snatched from my hand.

"*Food*, James. Not caffeine. You don't need coffee. You're a kid."

The man barely ever looked at me, but he always seemed to know exactly where I was. I waited until his back was turned before filling up a thermos and slipping it into my bag.

"You ready?" he asked impatiently, clicking off both phones and slipping them into his briefcase. "I'm giving you a ride in today."

I paused where I stood, giving him a strange look.

Since when do you care?

He seemed to ask himself the same question, but herded me towards the garage with an impatient wave. "Just get in the car."

When I say garage, it probably conjures a certain image. Two cars. Grease-stained floor. Cluttered shelves of personal memorabilia long ago surrendered to spiders.

Ours was different than that.

My father didn't seem to have much passion in his life, but one thing he did care about was his cars. He cared *fiercely*. Our garage had been custom-built to house four freakin' parking bays that were as long as the house. Shined like a showroom, and polished to the point where it was dangerous to walk on the floor.

There was the Porsche, the Benz, the Lamborghini, and something else so exclusively Italian that even I was unable to pronounce its name.

For a teenage boy, it was like living adjacent to a small piece of heaven. But under no circumstances was I allowed to touch. These cars belonged to my father. They were not for me. Ever.

He considered his choices for a split-second, and then unlocked the door to the Benz. I slid into the passenger seat and tossed my bag into the back, careful not to scratch the leather upholstery. The garage door came up, the phones were magically back, and he argued his way through two separate conversations as he shot backwards into the sun—almost killing the girl who lived next door in the process. I shot an apologetic glance over my shoulder but we were already speeding down the road towards the school, breaking every speed limit along the way.

There was only one high school in Seranto, California. A private school so ridiculously overpriced only the residents of the exclusive seaside community could afford to send their kids there. There was another school for the children of the working class twenty miles down the road.

None of us ever went there. We didn't even play them at sports.

The Benz pulled up beside several others as he dropped me in the student lot. Usually I'd be parking there myself, just a few spaces down. That meant walking home. No biggie, but he'd insisted on taking me in himself this morning. I was about to find out why.

"So I'm leaving tonight—catching the red-eye. Have to take a quick trip for work."

I wasn't sure if it was technically considered a 'red-eye' if it was on the company jet, but I admired his efforts to blend in with the common man. "How long will you be gone?"

The questions were routine by now. I'd asked them many times. "Two weeks."

I nodded robotically, and then it all suddenly clicked. The anemic display of guilt, the strange gesture of affection he was making by allowing me to ride in his precious car.

"I know you have that big game..." he preempted, distractedly running a hand through his hair. "We haven't been able to spend much time together lately. Sorry about that."

I didn't say anything. I was no longer expected to. I just nodded again—staring out the window at the entrance of the school. Wishing he would unlock the doors so I could leave. The neighbor girl came rushing along the sidewalk and into the school.

"Maybe we can go somewhere over the holidays," he offered, trying to sound friendly, infusing his voice with a false sense of cheer. "You're almost eighteen—that opens some doors. We could go to Budapest or Guam..."

Those were some pretty random places to choose for vacation. I swung my head back to look at him. I wondered if he had work there to do and I was just his excuse. Or more like his cover.

"Yeah, maybe." The bell rang and I reached for my bag and it over my shoulder, gripping the strap. "I have to go—don't want to be late."

"Right. Of course." The locks came up. "I'll see you soon, James."

"See ya."

I was mentally gone before my feet even hit the curb, walking across the pavement in long, sweeping strides, my thoughts a million miles away. Already fantasizing about my coffee and scrolling through a mental list of music, I about had a heart attack when he called out my name.

"James!"

I froze and then slowly turned around, wondering if I'd forgotten something in the car. He was leaning over the passenger seat, studying me carefully with the window rolled down. After a second of silence, all the hair started prickling on the back of my neck. Then he flashed me an unexpected smile.

"After your game...do something fun."

What the—? Something fun?

My lips parted as I stared at him in honest surprise. I couldn't remember the last time he'd suggested such a thing. Nor could I recall the last time he'd instructed me to do something just for me without having some bigger agenda. As I stared back at him, a strange kind of nostalgia started stirring deep in my chest. I had actually managed a smile in return by the time the car went tearing out of the parking lot, leaving me standing alone on the curb.

That's when the bell rang again, and I closed my eyes with a sigh.

...*late again.*

SERANTO HIGH MIGHT have been as rich as they come, but it was still high school. At some level, all high schools are pretty much the same.

You had the nerds, the jocks, the stoners, the student council. The hemp-only-vegans who scared away anyone who ventured too close to their table at lunch. Cut it open and the cross-section of every student population is exactly the same. All of them simply trying to keep their heads above water. All of them counting down the seconds till they could walk across that stage.

I was a jock. Blond hair, a spray of light freckles across my nose that I hated, and piercing blue eyes. Tall and athletic. Playing multiple sports, earning varsity letters in each. I wore my letterman jacket on Fridays and had been voted homecoming royalty since I was fourteen years old.

Before you start, I know the stereotype. I've heard it all before.

Teenage god. What some would call a privileged boy king. Living it up in his high school glory years, before the nerds and scholars rise to power in the years to come. The corporations of tomorrow were run by the techies and geeks of today, whereas jocks like me graduated then became promptly irrelevant if we didn't move on to the NFL, or NHL, or NBA, or some other professional league.

I didn't care how I looked. Didn't care that girls constantly messaged me. Didn't care that I had a body other guys wished they had. The thing is, I had no desire to play sports in college. And I had no intention of going to college anywhere in the same time zone as this insufferable little town. My dream? Gap year after high school, then pack a duffle bag and study abroad.

To study what? It didn't matter. Something with words, not numbers. I liked English and History. I was crap at math. The important thing wasn't the academics though, it was the distance. The way I figured, my dad would say no freakin' way to the gap year. But he'd embrace the idea of me going as far away as possible. I could only hope that the 'embracing' came with a financial assist.

"Dude—Jamie. How does this keep happening?"

I turned around and flashed a quick smile. Turns out I wasn't the only one late to school.

Kevin McConnell didn't exactly run in the upper echelons of high school society. He wasn't particularly good-looking, didn't have an exceptional amount of money or talent on the field. But what Kevin McConnell *did* have was access to his father's prescription pad.

For that reason alone Kevin was forever guaranteed a seat at the popular table, along with an invite to whatever party was being thrown that week. He was also asked to bring *snacks*.

Ironically, he was one of the only people worth talking to at those unbearable parties.

"We're a testament to the resilience of the human condition." I slapped his outstretched hand with a grin. "The confines of this craphole can't hold us."

"Naw, but its teachers can still throw us in detention."

The eyes were red and the words slightly slurred. Kevin's tardiness was usually on account of yesterday's booze and pill cocktail. I was surprised he'd made it in at all.

"Or should I say, they'll throw *me* in detention." He gave me a quick once-over. "Doesn't matter how late you are, Hunt. I don't see any of the faculty calling you on it."

"That's ridiculous." The two of us wandered reluctantly towards our first-period history class. The door was already closed and Mr. Dixon was monologuing like a Bond villain in the third act. "We're in this together. Sink or swim."

With that, we pushed open the door. And froze in the sudden spotlight.

"McConnell—you're *late*."

The word fired out like a bullet, leaving a trail of shrapnel in its wake. Dixon's sharp eyes swept right over me, fastening onto the baggy jeans and bloodshot retinas.

"Yes, sir." Kevin shifted uncomfortably, avoiding his probing gaze. "Jamie and I *both* missed the bell."

At this point, I couldn't begrudge him for trying. The favoritism was almost painful.

Sure enough, Dixon both acknowledged and dismissed me in the same instant.

"Hunt, take a seat. Don't let it happen again." He rounded with a vengeance on the other boy. "And *you*—you're lucky I don't give you a Breathalyzer right now. See me after class."

In this together, huh? Sink or swim?

Kevin shot me a sarcastic grin, which I returned with an innocent shrug. Then we took our seats as our teacher started up again.

It was a Thursday morning and the class was in its usual stupor. They'd tuned in just long enough to watch Dixon dole out his partisan punishment, and then sank back into a glassy-eyed daze.

My desk was in the very back of the room. Far enough away to escape attention, while being centrally located so as to gaze upon the whole dreary scene. Dixon was pontificating on economic growth trends of the 1920s, my buddy Max was making two Adderall chase each other across his desk, and the girl in front of me was distractedly chewing on her hair and secretly texting on her phone.

Riveting stuff. Really worth the forty grand it took to enroll here.

My mind blanked as I sank down further in my chair. Twirling a pencil between my fingers. Plotting how best to ask my father about a semester, or two, abroad.

Like most of the kids who lived in Seranto, I'd never had a job. Even if I'd expressed an interest, my father would never have allowed it. On the contrary, he would have thought it 'unseemly' for someone of our position. That was my dad. Fervently pretending to be American aristocracy, when the rest of the people who lived outside our zip code couldn't give a shit.

The pencil twirled faster and faster. It was taking on a life of its own.

It would help if I had something to contribute myself. Some sort of lousy pittance that would shine only in principle and help to coax his hand along.

Faster and faster the pencil twirled. The colors were just a blur of yellow now.

Maybe I could start tutoring after school. It's not like he could object to something like that, and at any rate it wasn't like he was ever going to find out—

"Mr. Hunt!"

My head snapped up as Dixon came to a stop right in front of my desk. His entire body was rigid, but in hindsight he was surprisingly calm considering the circumstances.

"Yes, sir?"

His eye twitched as the students behind him turned around to stare.

"Your pencil is on fire."

For a second, I just blinked. Then I glanced at the flaming embers in my hand.

"Shit!"

I dropped it with a yelp, shoving my chair away from the desk. Someone, I don't know who, threw their backpack on top of the flaming stick of wood on my desk, and within seconds it was nothing more than ash. There were just a few wisps of smoke to commemorate one of the strangest moments of my life.

What the hell?!

A terrifying hush fell over the classroom. No one moved. No one spoke. For a suspended moment, we all just sat there. Staring at the scorch mark in the center of my desk. Then, one by one, the rest of the class did what adolescents do best in moments of unexplained crisis.

They started laughing.

My head turned on a swivel, staring at nothing in particular, always coming back to the inexplicable mark. Someone clapped me on the shoulder. The laughter turned to applause. I wished I could strangle whoever started it. I wished I could get just one second to figure out—

"Hunt." I jumped out of my skin as Dixon's shadow loomed over me. "Care to tell me what's going on?"

That's a good question.

Was it a prank? Maybe it was a trick of the light? My eyes flickered about the room, searching for a guilty expression to clue me in. Nothing but blank faces. My heart picked up its hammering pace. My hands automatically curled into fists as they pressed against my jeans.

Then a throat cleared softly beside me.

"It's just a dumb lighter. Put it away, Jamie—stop wasting our time."

There was another chorus of laughter as Dixon stormed back to the front. No sooner had he gotten there than Kevin McConnell chimed in with an ill-timed, "I'm late two minutes and we're having a post-class therapy session. But James Hunt lights a pencil on fire..."

The entire class leapt on board, like lions zeroing in on a gazelle. A gazelle who at that very moment was probably asking himself why he'd spent an additional two years in a masters program just for the 'privilege' of teaching us deplorable kids.

I waited for them to get into it. Waited for enough eyes to swivel back to the front. Then I cast a side glance at the brown-haired girl sitting beside me.

She alone wasn't participating in the recreational crucifixion. She was staring at a deep gouge in her desk, tracing the edges of it with the tip of her nail. I watched, transfixed for a moment, and then leaned over as discreetly as I could.

"Thanks for saying that."

The finger came to a pause, though her eyes stayed glued to the desk.

"What do you mean?"

I hazarded a quick look towards Dixon, then leaned farther over. Lowering my voice.

"About the lighter. Thanks for covering for me."

Those eyes came up, and all of a sudden I found myself caught in their piercing glare.

"Covering for you?" She cocked her head to the side, looking at me with the strangest expression I had ever seen. "You used a lighter, didn't you? How else would you start the fire?"

My heart quickened, my face froze, and every possible excuse I could think of went flying out the window. I cast a final look at the burn on my desk before retracting my fingers.

"Yeah...I used a lighter."

Chapter 2

By second period, the entire school had heard how James Hunt lit a pencil on fire in the back of his history class. By fourth period, he was dripping gasoline on the desk and challenging Dixon to a duel. But then, at lunchtime, Ashley Hudston got caught with a joint in the girls' locker room and the entire pencil incident was forgotten.

"Yo, Jamie!" a varsity linebacker called from across the hall. "You think I should take Clayton's quiz in bio, or just set the whole thing on fire?"

Okay...it was *almost* forgotten.

I flashed him a weak smile, taking advantage of the flurry caused by the bell to duck into the bathroom unnoticed. It was the first moment I'd had to myself since walking into school, and after carefully checking to make sure the stalls were empty I let out a deep breath and stared down at my hands.

What the hell happened back there?

I put both hands on of the sink, leaning towards the mirror. There was nothing unusual about my reflection. Nothing that screamed 'boy who magically incinerates writing implements with his bare hands'. I was nothing but a high school senior who was, again, late to class.

This couldn't have been *me*, right? There had to be some other explanation.

"Planning your next pyrotechnic display?"

I jumped back with a start as the door opened and a leggy blonde slipped inside. She locked it behind her, flashing a perfectly practiced grin as the florescent lights played with the highlights in her hair.

"Did you miss the sign?" I joked with a tight smile, knowing full well she hadn't. Alicia Cartwright had been trying to get me alone since the beginning of term. I'd avoided her thus far. Up till now.

She ignored the question, sliding in between me and the sink.

"You've been avoiding me."

Not a question.

"I haven't," I said quickly, suddenly feeling too warm.

She leaned back onto her elbows, staring up at me with a smile. "You're also a terrible liar."

Also not a question. She had a way of doing that. She also had a point about the lying.

Like most of the people in this town, Alicia and I had basically grown up together. Sat in the same classroom since we were in kindergarten. Attended the same school dances, oftentimes together. Snuck away on our fourth-grade field trip to smoke cigarettes until we both got sick.

The quarterback and the cheerleader was a nauseating cliché, but it didn't matter when your graduating class had fewer than a hundred people. We made out the first time in fifth grade. Went farther than that in junior high. Got caught naked in the hot tub by my dad our freshman year. Nothing was ever serious enough to stick, but now, apparently, she wanted to try again.

I raked my hair back with a sigh, giving up before I'd even started. "I'm not avoiding you, Alicia, I swear. I'm just..."

"...just not interested in carrying on a high school fling when we're both off to college next year? Yeah, I get that." She peeled herself away from the sink, closing the distance I'd discreetly placed between us. "But if you think we're not hooking up this year, you're out of your mind."

The shameless audacity produced a genuine grin.

"You know it's not *just* up to you, right?"

She leaned up onto her toes and kissed me squarely on the mouth, her tongue slipping in to brush mine. She leaned back slightly. "You know the final bell rang, like, five minutes ago, right?"

The grin faded as my eyes flew to the door. "It did...?"

Thirsty seconds later I was sliding into my English class, wincing an apologetic grimace to my teacher, Ms. Braun, before I took my seat in the back. Thankfully, she spared me a censure and continued explaining a handout she'd given to the class. I stole an extra one off the desk of the person sitting across from me and pulled out a pencil.

Then I carefully put the same pencil back in my bag.

Better safe than sorry.

"—not due for another two weeks, but *do not* procrastinate on this one," Braun was wrapping up. "I promise, I'm not going to take 'but it was homecoming' as an excuse."

There was an obligatory groan from the students but, generally speaking, everyone was in fine spirits. The second she stopped talking they erupted into a cheerful sort of chaos, dragging their desks across the linoleum and chattering about tomorrow's game.

I froze uncertainly, wishing very much I hadn't missed the first five minutes of class.

"Playing catch-up, Mr. Hunt?" Ms. Braun wove her way back to my desk with a chiding frown. "I wonder why that is."

A few years ago, the school board took a vote and declared that teachers were no longer allowed to call us by our first names. It was meant to be a sign of respect. A 'treat them as adults, and they'll act as adults' sort of thing. Little did they know how much condescension the faculty at Seranto High was able to infuse in those few respectful syllables.

"I'm sorry," I apologized immediately. "I've been having an off—weird day."

That was one way of putting it.

"So I've heard." She flashed me a knowing smile, probably grateful I'd kept the lighter in my pocket, then gestured to the petite girl beside her. "You have a project on Gatsby due in two weeks. Miss Tanner here will be your partner. She can fill you in on everything you missed."

Gabrielle Tanner. Guess I was being punished after all.

The sentiment must have shown on my face because Braun smiled, and I could have sworn I heard her mutter 'you snooze, you lose' before walking away.

Great. Just great.

Gabrielle Tanner didn't fit into your average high school chronicles.

She was near the top of our class, but wasn't in the honor's society. She had just as much money as the rest of us, but never attended the same parties. And even though she was damn beautiful, she sat by herself at lunch. No sports teams. Definitely not the cheerleader type either. Kinda on the weird side, but not really weird. If that made any sense.

An adolescent enigma, but it wasn't entirely unwarranted. We kept our distance from her just as much as she kept her distance from us.

"Cool," I said with as much enthusiasm as I could muster, gesturing to an open chair. I could only imagine how quickly everyone else had paired up, leaving her all alone. "So what's this big project?"

"Dual perspective essay," she said without inflection, sinking into the chair. "The unwritten letters between Daisy and Gatsby. First draft is due on Monday."

Monday? This coming Monday... really?

"Shit," I cursed under my breath, casting a fleeting glare at the teacher. "Only Braun would assign us something the weekend after a big game."

Gabrielle stared at me for a second, then dropped her eyes to the desk with something close to disgust. "How original," she muttered. "A self-involved jock."

My eyes flashed up and I bristled at the stereotype. "How predictable: a judgmental loner."

As soon as I said the words, I felt guilty. It wasn't in my nature to lash out like that. If anything, growing up with my dad had taught me to avoid confrontation at all costs. In truth, I didn't have anything against Gabrielle. The avoidance was a pack mentality—nothing personal.

I'd actually had a crush on her in the fifth grade. But it only lasted a few weeks before I'd fallen in love with our science teacher, Miss Calvenetti.

"Sorry," I muttered. "I don't know why I said that."

She stared at me for a second, and then apparently decided to let it go. "Let's just get this over with." She opened her book, dreading the assignment just as much as me. "The more we get done now, the less likely we'll have to meet outside of class."

My eyebrows lifted ever so slightly, and I fought the sudden urge to smile. The most popular girl in school jumped me in the bathroom not ten minutes ago, and this lovely pariah was cursing her luck at being forced to be my English partner.

Women.

"Wouldn't want that," I answered sweetly, opening my book as well.

While the rest of the class goofed around for the majority of the period—pretending to concentrate only when Ms. Braun made her occasional rotation through the aisles—Gabrielle and I worked in steady silence until the bell.

She was smart. Picking out stylistic quirks and themes with ease before paring them down into an efficient outline. She seemed surprised that I had brains as well—which I couldn't help resenting. Each time I'd contribute an idea of my own, she'd look up with a start before reluctantly adding it to the page. When it became clear I'd already finished reading the book she'd looked at me with downright suspicion, like she was convinced I was pulling some sort of prank.

The hour dragged by at a glacial pace, and when the bell rang for us to start packing up our supplies I actually leaned back with a sigh of relief. "Well, that was excruciating."

She shot me a quick glance, surprised by my unexpected honestly, and her face melted into a disturbingly sweet smile. "Sorry, I was in a much better mood this morning, before your dad almost *ran me over with his car.*"

My eyes flashed up, then darkened with sincere remorse. I remembered the look on her face as we'd shot out of the driveway. The surprise, anger then, finally, the sullen resentment.

"Yeah, I...sorry about that. My dad can be a little—"

"I know exactly who your dad is," she snapped.

Of course she did. The whole country knew who my dad was.

"Yeah, sorry," I said again, feeling like I'd spent the entire morning apologizing for things that weren't entirely my fault. "At any rate, it feels like we got most of it done today. Maybe just one outside session and we'll have it finished."

She nodded, looking pleased. "Want to meet on Saturday? My parents are gone, so we'd have the house to ourselves."

I started nodding automatically, then stopped myself with a guilty flush. "Actually...a bunch of us were heading to the beach on Saturday." There was an awkward pause. "You should come," I added half-heartedly.

Her lips twisted up into a hard smile. "Thanks, but I'll leave you to it."

Which elicited an even more awkward pause.

"How's tomorrow?" I suggested quickly.

"Sure." The second bell rang and she slung the strap of her bag across her shoulder. "I'll be home after school. Come by whenever."

"Cool." I grabbed my bag as well. "I'll see you—"

But she was already gone.

"—then."

My forehead creased with a frown as I gazed after her, wondering what might possibly be going on behind those defensive eyes. I was still staring at the empty doorway when a heavy hand clamped down on my shoulder, startling me out of my trance.

"Dude, you got stuck with Tanner? That sucks."

Matt Harris, one of my teammates and regular partners in crime, joined me in the back of the room. Jack Walsh and Dave Lipinski were at his side.

"Honestly, I'd complain to Braun," he continued. "Ask if you can just do it alone."

Jack grinned, tossing his copy of the book into the air. "Or you could just set it on fire..."

I gave him a playful shove as Dave plopped down on my desk, staring at the door where Gabrielle had just disappeared. "Nah, man, you're lucky. Setting up little study dates at Gabrielle Tanner's house..." He grunted like he'd just tasted something incredibly delicious. "I don't care how psycho she is—the girl is *fine*."

"You should definitely hit that before graduation," Matt agreed, reneging on his former position. "Just for the life experience."

"Dude!" Jack was scandalized. "*She'd* probably set *him* on fire!"

An image of her face flashed in my mind. Dark hair, wide hazel eyes staring up at me with the barest hint of a smile playing around her lips.

"Leave it alone," I said briskly, herding them out the door. "Let's just get to practice."

Truth be told, I'd always felt the slightest bit protective of Gabrielle Tanner. Not because she was quiet, or antisocial, or unnaturally pretty for someone so shy. It was for a simple reason.

She was my neighbor.

"YOU THINK THAT'S GOING TO CUT IT? SERIOUSLY! IF
YOU KIDS LOSE THIS GAME, YOU'RE GOING TO REGRET
IT FOR THE REST OF YOUR LIVES!"

Football coaches had a way of keeping things in perspective.

"AGAIN, YOU CRETINS! AGAIN!"

I waited for the receivers to get back into place, distractedly tossing
the ball back and forth in my hands. We might have been less than
twenty-four hours before the semi-finals, a game I'd been waiting my
entire varsity career to play, but my head was a thousand miles away.

Strangely enough, even though my day had been a series of unfor-
tunate events, it wasn't any of those things that had my attention. Not
the flaming pencil, or the bathroom kiss, or the Gatsby project, or even
the fact that my dad had given me a random ride to school. It was a children's nursery tale. One my mother used to read to me before I went to
sleep.

The story of a kid who woke up every night and found himself in
the middle of the woods. Night after night this happened, until one day
he realized that his world was upside-down. That he'd only dreamt he'd
fallen asleep. That he'd lived in the woods the whole time.

In hindsight, that's a creepy thing to read to a kid...

"YOU CALL THAT A THROW, HUNT? MY GRAND-
MOTHER COULD THROW BETTER THAN THAT, AND
SHE'S BEEN DEAD FOR THIRTY YEARS!"

I startled back to attention just in time to see the ball I'd robotically
thrown sail right over the hands of the receiver. He was tackled with a
sickening crunch, and the defense cheered.

"Sorry, Nate!"

Nate Jessup flipped me off with a good-natured grin, and then
limped back into position. Fortunately the coach called for a break, and
he was able to shake off the concussion in peace.

"Dude, everything okay?" Matt yanked off his helmet and trotted over to me, sweaty curls plastered to the sides of his face. "What's up with you?"

I shook back to the present quickly, burying the bedtime story deep in the recesses of my mind. "Haven't you heard?" I gestured to where our coach was having a mild coronary by the water cooler. "I've dishonored my family name."

Matt chuckled. "Yeah, he's worse than usual. Before we came out here, I saw him hyperventilating into a paper bag in his car."

"He does that every Thursday," I said dismissively. "Most of it is court-ordered, but I think he came up with the meditation tapes on his own."

He laughed again then snatched the ball from my hands, holding it tauntingly out of reach. "Seriously though, man, you better get it together. I've got a lot riding on this game."

"Oh yeah?" I made a swipe for the ball and missed, relieved to be talking about something normal. "Do tell."

"Lauren," he said simply, tossing it back and forth with a grin. "If we win tomorrow night, she promised to be in a...celebratory mood."

I laughed, leaping high into the air and snatching the ball back for good. "In that case, I'll do my best. The world knows your hand could use a break."

He jumped on top of me with a shout, trying to tear it out of my hands. The three guys standing closest to us were quick to join in, and before long we were locked in an impromptu battle. Laughing, cursing, and pummeling each other without remorse, until—

A white van pulled around the corner and everyone froze.

I guess it shouldn't have bothered me. I guess after all this time I should have gotten used to the sight of them. After all, most of those vans belonged to my father.

The story was simple enough.

It was a genetic anomaly. An evolutionary glitch that, if left unchecked, would fester and spread. I remembered seeing it on the news. There was a girl only a few years older than me getting dragged out of her school by unsmiling men with guns. I was too young to understand what was happening; too young to know what the newscaster meant when he used words like 'quarantine' and 'purge'.

In my mind, the idea of 'supernatural abilities' was straight out of a movie. Like the kind of thing that the hero would use to save the planet and blow the bad guys away. I'd been terribly excited about the revelation that these things were actually real. I remembered drawing pictures of myself in crayon with superpowers of my own. Those drawings were quickly destroyed.

It wasn't until a few years later that I came to understand the ramifications of those fateful headlines. That I came to realize our nation had decided it was under attack. People instinctively feared what they couldn't understand, and they instinctively hated what they feared.

A special task force was commissioned. The kind with limited governmental oversight and virtually limitless funding. That's when the purge began. Ten years ago those people with special abilities were rounded up, vanished into a black hole. Five years later, the gene was supposedly isolated and their mothers were rounded up as well.

Since then, hardly a week would go by without hearing another story on the news. The systematic genocide of the supernatural race became our nation's favorite pastime and people would sit in front of their television screens for hours every night, waiting for the next person to get outed. Waiting for some teenager to get dragged out of their house, never to be seen again.

We were supposed to be grateful. We were supposed to feel safe.

In my case, I was supposed to be proud. Because those white vans, the ones that rolled silently down the streets looking for prey, the ones that made the hair on the back of my neck stand on end...those white vans answered to my father.

Lucky me.

The ball went limp in my hands as the group of us straightened up, staring silently until the van disappeared at the end of the street. We stared long after it had left. Quiet and still.

"How about that," Matt murmured, shivering in spite of himself. "Looks like your dad is hard at work."

I swallowed back bile, shuddering at what might be on the news that night. "Yeah, looks like he is..."

Dave coughed, and a laugh that sounded forced followed. "He's probably picking up half the team we're playing. Wants his son to win no matter the cost."

"Yeah, no matter the cost," I said, staring at the football in my hands.

Chapter 3

School the next day was a wash. A Thursday just like it always was before every big game. Like trying to make kids sit still the day before Christmas break. Football was a way of life for these people.

Football and money.

I got through my classes quickly and without incident. Without incident meaning nothing spontaneously turned to ash or caught on fire. Whatever had happened was clearly a figment of my imagination. I must've done something or someone had done something to my pencil and just hadn't told me yet. It didn't matter, since no one cared anymore anyway. We were all focused on the game. The teachers had no expectations of us and assigned no homework. So it was with a clear schedule that I swept outside five minutes ahead of the bell and sped all the way home, looking forward to an empty house and pizza delivery.

There was just one thing I had to do first.

Well, this should be interesting...

At four-thirty on the dot I stepped onto my front porch, staring with trepidation at the house next door. It was almost exactly like mine: two-stories with an attic. Painted cream with a gabled roof, and the same ostentatious framework as the rest of the mini-mansions on the block.

The only difference was the trees. While every other house in the neighborhood boasted manicured gardens and meticulously trimmed lawns, the Tanners' house was half-hidden by an enormous grove of trees. I'd heard my dad rant about it once, threatening to lodge a complaint with the homeowners' association. But I liked the trees. I'd often imagined how it must feel from the inside. Safely concealed from prying eyes.

Why I was being so punctual, I didn't know. Gabrielle had said she'd be home all day; it wasn't like we'd scheduled a proper time. But something about those hazel eyes of hers had put me on notice. Made me feel unnervingly formal, like I should arrive with a gift.

Dude, she can probably see you right now. Just go over there already.

In times of crisis, the voice in my head tended to alienate me. Call it self-preservation. He preferred to watch from a distance and judge.

Feeling like a bit of an idiot, I pulled in a deep breath and then jogged across my front lawn to the sidewalk. Rather than cut through the small forest her parents called a garden, I slowed my pace and stayed carefully on the walkway, shooting curious glances to the side the whole time.

I'd swear the temperature dropped ten degrees. Must be all that glorious shade.

My backpack hung low on a shoulder as I cleared my throat then rang the bell. Again, I had no idea why I was so nervous. While things might have been awkward at school, Gabrielle and I had lived next door to each other since we were about two years old. It wasn't the first time I'd been over to her house. Her mom used to babysit me until my dad got home from work.

It *was* the first time I'd been here since learning to speak in complete sentences, however. Between that and learning to use the toaster, my dad figured I could pretty much be left on my own.

There was movement on the other side of the door. I heard a cabinet closing. Feet were pounding on the stairs. Somewhere in the house, the music that had been playing turned off. The Arctic Monkeys or Radiohead. Something that was too far away to hear. Something I was sure I'd listened to myself.

"Oh—hey." She pulled open the door and greeted me all in one breath. "Perfect timing, I just got back from a run."

She was obviously not feeling the same sense of formality as me. Her school clothes had been replaced with yoga pants and a fitted tank.

Her hair was damp from a shower and hung in loose waves down her back. Little spirals of coconut-scented steam were still rising from her skin, and her bare feet were tapping impatiently on the carpet.

I took the hint and stepped inside.

"You run?" I asked before I could stop myself.

Obviously. Idiot.

She gave me a blank stare. "No, I was just texting *really* fast."

Our eyes met as a flush of embarrassment froze me in my tracks. Time stalled a moment, then she seemed to take pity on me and gestured towards the living room with a little grin.

"Actually, I was about to order pizza. You want some?"

I dropped my bag onto the sofa and glanced back with pleasant surprise. There was only one place in town close enough to deliver, and considering how many nights my dad was away on business I'd come to know every employee by name.

"Yeah, that sounds great."

Her fingers dialed the number by memory. "Hawaiian—"

"—is terrible. I hope that's a joke."

She stared at me while the phone rang, then very ostentatiously ordered half-Hawaiian and half-whatever football players like to eat. I listened with a little smile, pretending not to be paying attention as I made a quick study of the room. It was messy. But it was a teenage kind of messy. I suddenly wondered how long her parents had been away.

"Done." She hung up the phone and plopped down onto the sofa, pulling out her notes at the same time. "Should be here in fifteen minutes."

I nodded, then gestured to a family portrait on the wall. "How long have your parents been gone?"

The Tanners were both consultants for some big tech firm that was based in London. The company had offices on six continents, and they were often away for weeks at a time.

Her eyes followed mine, and she hesitated for just a split second before pulling out a pencil with a teasing smile. "Is this going to be safe around you? Or should I get a crayon?"

I chuckled in spite of myself, settling down on the cushion beside her. "I think we can risk it. Better your house than mine."

We shared a genuine smile, then dropped our eyes quickly and pulled out our books. This was not a social visit. There were things to get done. After which, I'd be leaving immediately.

For the next fifteen minutes, we worked in silence. It wasn't as awkward as it could have been, partially because she got up halfway through and turned on the music that had been playing before. I was right, it was Radiohead. I had the poster for the album taped to my wall.

Our heads bobbed up and down to the music as our pencils flew across the page. It was a little daunting, trying to keep up with her, but in the end I was proud of what I'd done.

It wasn't until we exchanged papers that we realized we had a problem.

"You're writing as Gatsby?" I asked in surprise, looking up from her draft. We had never expressly assigned the roles of Daisy versus Gatsby. I'd just assumed...

"Wait—you are, too?" She snatched up my paper, and then her face fell with a sigh. "Shit."

I froze in complete bewilderment. "Of course I'm writing as him, why the hell are you?"

"Gatsby's the more interesting character," she said without hesitation.

"He's also the *guy*." I set her paper down, torn between amusement and exasperation. "If we're supposed to be writing letters as this couple, I just assumed that—"

"That, what?" she challenged. "That I'd have to write the boring female perspective?"

"Well...yeah."

Her eyes narrowed slightly, but she didn't back down. Quite the contrary, she fixed me with another dangerously saccharine smile. The kind I'd already learned to fear.

"Tell you what...why don't we just read through the drafts, and whoever did a better job can keep the character. Agreed?"

Game changer.

Growing up with my dad had taught me the value of a bluff, but I was a flat-out terrible liar. Instead of trying I kept my face free of emotion, handing back her paper with a shrug.

"You can keep Gatsby," I said graciously. "I don't have a problem writing the girl."

Just being a gentleman. It had absolutely nothing to do with the fact that your paper is better than mine.

"You sure?" she pressed, taunting me. "I'd be happy to read over what you wrote."

I snatched the copy out of her hands and stuffed it into my bag. If she'd tried to retrieve it, I honestly think I might have swallowed the thing. Neither of us said a word as we returned to our work. But when she glanced up at me a minute later, I could have sworn I saw a smile.

That's when the doorbell rang.

Thank the Maker.

I set down my book with a sigh of relief, reaching automatically for my wallet to help with the bill. "Here, let me get this."

"No, it's cool." She was already halfway to the door, pulling a folded stack of bills from a wooden chest in the entryway. "If we do this again, you can get the next one."

If we do this again.

My head snapped up and I found myself staring after her without really knowing why. A moment later she reappeared, balancing a giant cardboard box in her hands.

"As promised." She set it on the sofa between us, pulling out a greasy slice. "Enjoy."

I followed her motions carefully, glancing down at the leather cushions. "Won't your parents mind? You want me to grab some plates?"

My dad would straight-up murder me if I ate pizza on the couch. Under no circumstances was food allowed to leave the kitchen. Our house was a pristine testament to that rule.

Again, there was an almost imperceptible pause before Gabrielle answered the question.

"It's fine, they're pretty laid-back." But she tossed me a napkin before gesturing to the box. "At any rate, they're on the other side of the Atlantic. We're safe."

I nodded, and reached for the box, trying to shake the feeling that, at any moment, a SWAT team would drop down from the sky. "Half-Hawaiian and half-football, huh?"

She swallowed loudly and flashed me a grin.

"The guy interpreted that as meat-lover's. Go figure."

I let out a laugh and then suddenly fell quiet, feeling rather off-balance.

This wasn't what I expected when I came over here. Laughing over pizza. Joking around while listening to Radiohead. This wasn't what I expected at all.

My eyes flickered up and I found myself watching her—curious, in spite of my better judgment. Picking up on all those things I'd missed. Little details I'd never noticed before.

To be honest, it was hard to get past the face. The face was almost too pretty. It demanded attention. Then there was the body. She could hide it beneath as many t-shirts as she wanted, but I was a teenage guy. Our brains were highly adept at this sort of thing. Her body was perfection. She was slender, at times almost delicate, but with just enough curves to catch my eye.

Yes, it was hard to get past those things. But once I did, I found my-self unable to look away. Drawn in by the fascinating quirks and tells that she didn't seem aware of herself.

The way she played out the melody to whatever song we were lis-tening to on her right leg. The way she immediately grabbed a second slice of pizza after she'd finished scarfing down her first. The way she'd answered the door with no makeup, fresh from a shower.

That alone was enough to blow me away. The last time I'd seen a girl without makeup had been when me and some of the guys crashed Melanie Horton's birthday party in the eighth grade, and even then all the girls had run screaming from the room.

There was something genuine about her that caught me by surprise. It was a complete lack of pretension that was something of an anomaly in the adolescent world.

"Hey creep, I asked you a question."

She's also staring right at me.

My gaze dropped to the sofa, and I blushed guiltily before hesitant-ly looking at her face again. Sure enough, she was staring like I'd had a fit or something. I was quick to clear my face. "Sorry—what?"

"I asked if you wanted some ranch." She fought back a smile. "Un-less you'd like to continue thinking of all the ways you could kill me."

I ignored this last part, silently cursing myself for staring so long. "Ranch?" I repeated with a frown, sure I'd heard wrong. "On the piz-za?"

"Yeah, on the pizza." She pushed to her feet and ducked into the kitchen to grab a bottle from the fridge. "How is it possible that you've never had that?"

I watched in morbid fascination as she squirted a dollop onto her slice, licking the drops on her fingers. "...because it's gross?"

"Try some."

By now, I should have expected it. But that didn't mean I had to play along.

"Absolutely not." I lifted my own slice to my mouth, taking a huge bite as she wielded the bottle like a weapon. "Put that down."

Her lips twitched up into a mocking grin. "Come on...Seranto High's star quarterback is too scared to try a bite of ranch?"

Why am I smiling? This isn't...why the heck am I smiling?

"While the parallels you draw between football and salad dressing are fascinating, I'm going to pass. Seriously, just looking at it is enough to make me—"

A splash hit me right in the face.

"—sick."

To be fair, it wasn't exactly her fault. She'd aimed for the pizza at the precise moment I'd lowered the slice to my napkin. But those technicalities didn't make much of a difference when streams of thick white dressing were dripping down my neck.

"Oh crap!" Her hands clapped over her mouth as her eyes widened to perfect saucers. "I can't believe...Jamie, I'm so sorry! I can't believe I just did that!"

I was frozen perfectly still. Stunned into silence.

"Please, say something!" She was starting to panic now, dabbing frantically with a napkin at my nose and neck. "I-I know that looked intentional, but I swear I really didn't do it on—"

My pizza smashed into her face.

"—purpose."

I was grinning again. In fact, I couldn't seem to stop. The longer she sat there, smeared with bacon and marinara, the worse it got. By the time she finally looked up at me, little drops of ranch dressing clinging to her eyelashes, I was shaking with silent laughter.

"I *did* do it on purpose," I clarified. "Just in case there was any confusion."

She gave me a hard stare, and then nodded slowly. Her mouth opened, but before she could say anything a glob of cheese fell off her face and onto the floor.

We both stared at it. Then bowed our heads at the same time.

And *that's* why we only eat in the kitchen...

I GUESS I COULD HAVE gone back to my house, but I didn't. Instead I found myself standing in Gabrielle Tanner's bathroom, washing salad dressing from my hair.

Weirdest. Week. Ever.

We hadn't really said anything after it happened, just shifted our school supplies aside and got to work cleaning up the mess. She'd pointed silently to the kitchen, and I returned with paper towels and water. The rest of the pizza was stored safely in the fridge.

Once cleaned, we'd quarantined ourselves to separate sides of the house. I was instructed to clean up in this bathroom, while she vanished into a room at the other end of the hall.

She wasn't throwing me out, so that was a good sign. She hadn't slapped me either, which was surprising. To be honest, she seemed to be having the same problem as me.

Angry. Uncomfortable. But...trying not to smile?

I dried my face on a washcloth then stared at my reflection in the mirror, shaking back my damp hair. How had she gotten so much ranch on me? I blinked and stared at my face, wondering at the feverish glow around my eyes. Had they always been so blue, or was it just weird lighting? Maybe it was the ranch. Maybe I was having some kind of allergic—

"Jamie?"

I pulled back with a start and then cleared my throat quickly, grabbing my shirt out of the sink and pulling it over my head. "Yeah, come in."

The door opened and Gabrielle hovered uncertainly in the hallway, watching as I raked my hair out of my eyes. She'd changed into pajama shorts and a thin sweater. It clung to her collarbone, dipping every so often as she tugged nervously on the sleeves.

"Listen, I'm really sorry about earlier." A long ponytail trailed down one shoulder as she bowed her head. "I was just messing around; I never meant to...anyways, I'm sorry."

"Hey, it was *funny*." I took a step forward, leaning down to catch her eye. "And yours was just an accident. If anyone should be apologizing, it's me. And that's something I have no intention of doing. Not after you decided to make me re-write my entire English assignment."

She snorted in laughter, then tentatively lifted her eyes. My entire face warmed with a grin, and before I knew what was happening I blurted the first thing that popped into my head.

"You really should come this weekend. To the beach."

It was like the air got sucked out of the room. All those good feelings melted away in a single instant. Her face went cold and she took a sudden step back.

"We both know why I can't do that."

The smile slid off my face and I took a step back as well.

Yeah, we do.

It had happened a few years ago—the spring of our freshman year. A bunch of us were at a house party when Gabrielle had too much to drink. She started freaking out in the bathroom, screaming and crying. It went on so long that a neighbor eventually called the cops. They had to break down the door just to get her out. By the time they did, she was passed out on the floor.

She'd been one of the most popular kids at Seranto High, but a police intervention was too scandalous to simply shrug off and the student population wasn't that forgiving. The people who'd gone to the party with her weren't talking to her by the time it was through. The friends who usually sat at her lunch table had conveniently relocated the next day at school.

Just like that, Gabrielle Tanner became a living ghost. Banished to the periphery of the student collective. Forced to live out the rest of her high school days in exile.

And just like that...our sunny afternoon had come to an end.

"I should go," I said quietly, bowing my head to avoid her gaze.

Those hazel eyes tightened with some uncertain emotion, but it was gone before I could see. Instead she nodded briskly, heading back down the stairs. I followed her down and packed my things quickly, hyperaware of the fact that she was waiting by the door.

She pulled it open the second I got close, a clear indication to leave.

"Well...thanks for the pizza," I murmured, fiddling awkwardly with the strap of my bag.

"'Bye, Jamie."

Ouch.

With a tight smile and a nod I slipped past her through the door, a bit surprised to see how low the sun had already fallen in the sky. I'd planned on staying less than an hour. Had it been longer than that? Resisting the urge to glance at my watch, I moved swiftly down the walkway and out past the trees. My pace quickened the second I cleared them, and I was already halfway back to my house before I heard her calling my name.

"Jamie!" I turned around in surprise as she went flying up the trail, waving something in her hand. It wasn't until she got closer that I realized what it was. "You forgot your book."

She slapped it into my chest without really looking at me and turned to walk away, only pausing when the pencil that had been marking my page clattered to the ground. A strange look flitted across her face as she picked it up, giving it a long stare before pressing it into my hand.

"You should be careful with this," she said quietly. "The kids at our school have a long memory...even the good ones."

With that, she left me standing alone on the porch.

Feeling like I'd been slapped in the face.

Chapter 4

Game day.

Every Friday morning, I woke up feeling exactly the same way. *Electrified.* Like the sun had risen just for the occasion. Like the air was buzzing with some invisible current, a whisper of excitement that made it hard to pull in a full breath.

Every Friday morning, it was exactly the same...except today.

My alarm screeched and I sat up slowly, reaching out to silence it before raking back my tangled hair. A sudden smell of coconut scented the air around me and I stared down at my hands with a frown before remembering where it had come from. The tiny glass bottle in Gabrielle Tanner's bathroom. Everything in there was coconut. Right down to the soap, the shampoo, and the row of tea lights that lined the edge of the tub. I'd made a cursory investigation the second I walked in there. Snooping around with the curiosity of a guy who'd lived next door for seventeen years.

A quiet sigh hunched my shoulders as I lifted my eyes to the window, staring blankly at the wall of trees guarding the house next door. From here, I could just barely see the curtains inside her window. Barely hear the faint strains of music as she got ready for school.

Snap out of it! Game day!

Sometimes that voice in my head had a point. It was Friday morning, after all. And this wasn't just any game, it was the semi-finals. I was the starting quarterback this year.

Pushing the melancholy face of Gabrielle Tanner safely from my mind, I leapt out of bed and stepped into the shower. The jets of hot water soothed the tension in my shoulders, replacing any sweet hint of coconut with the much stronger scent of my body wash. The smell steadied me, focused me. Tilted my world back to center as I hurried through the rest of my routine.

Like most things, it was easier with my dad away. I scarfed down a bowl of the world's most sugary cereal, and then filled my thermos of coffee to the brim before heading toward the garage. His cars were tempting—unbearably tempting—but I bypassed them the same as usual and climbed into my jeep instead. The garage door opened slowly, giving me plenty of time to cast covetous glances at the Porsche, but my father was a careful man. There wasn't a doubt in my mind that he had the mileage recorded. And I didn't want to imagine what might happen if I was caught.

With the windows down and music blaring, I shot out of the driveway and rocketed onto the street...only to come to a sudden pause.

Should I offer her a ride to school?

The question froze me in place, idling nervously in front of her house. It wasn't necessary of course, both of us lived close enough to walk, but why not offer anyway? We'd smashed food in each other's faces hours before—would a ride to school be so much of a stretch?

Then that voice piped up, mocking and cruel.

You've been sitting here for a full minute.

Without a backward glance I took off down the street, shaking off any last semblances of curiosity or guilt as I headed full speed for Seranto High. There was a game to win.

And they couldn't win that game without me.

ON SECOND THOUGHT, maybe we can't win this game at all...

My hands flew up in front of my face, just as a three-hundred-pound linebacker tackled me around the waist, smashing my body into the ground. All the air rushed out of my chest in a broken gasp as my shoulder blades cratered six inches into the sod.

"Third down!"

Instead of getting up I lay there, stunned senseless. Trying to recover even a modicum of feeling in my legs. We'd been hearing all week that Coralto Hills was a tough team, especially in terms of defense. But we'd had no idea that their defense had been feasting on steroids and ale.

"Jamie, you okay?!"

Matt pulled himself out of the tangle of bodies on the field, kneeling quickly by my side. With his help I was able to pull off my helmet, twisting my head to spit out a mouthful of blood. Slowly, my vision cleared. His face sharpened back into focus.

"...who's Jamie?" I sat up with a wince, rubbing the back of my neck as the Goliath who'd tackled me trotted back to his team, chortling under his breath. It was the fifth time he'd attempted to take my life. Under normal circumstances, that gave a quarterback the right to set fire to the men who were supposed to be defending him. But these weren't normal circumstances, and I could hardly blame my own team. There was simply no physical way to stop the guy.

"That's the spirit." He helped me to my feet, grimacing sympathetically at the steady drip of blood leaking down from my hair. "You might want to cover that up. They'll make you leave the field."

Wouldn't want that.

With a scathing glare I wiped my face clean with the back of my hand, following him over to the huddle, where our legendary team was looking decidedly worse for wear.

"Jamie, I'm so sorry, dude!" A heavy hand clapped on my back as Jeremy Roth, the fullback who was supposed to protect me from getting blitzed, hung his head in defeat. Both sides of his face were heavily bruised, and I could only imagine what damage the rest of his body had sustained. "I swear I'm trying, but that guy keeps—"

"Don't worry about it." Jeremy was the biggest guy I knew, but the Coralto Hills giant still had a good fifty pounds on him. "The guy's built like a tank."

There was a grumble of assent as the rest of the team gathered on the field, frozen in the final seconds of the game, waiting for whatever Shakespearean-style pep-talk our lunatic coach had drummed up on the sidelines.

As usual, he didn't disappoint. I could practically hear the swell of an invisible orchestra as the man stepped onto the grass.

"Hear me now...for I shall not say it twice." He paced between us like a seasoned general. Hands clenched into fists. His eyes were sparking with the heat of battle. Completely oblivious to the cart selling popcorn and cotton candy behind his back. "The men who came before you fought bravely on this field. The grass on which you stand has grown from their tears and blood. But they did not fight for nothing. They did not do battle upon this hallowed ground in vain."

There was a throbbing pulse near his temple. He was about four seconds from a stroke.

"Tonight...we honor their memory! Tonight...*we take back what is ours!*"

On that ringing note, he turned on his heel and marched straight off the field. Assumedly to listen to the remainder of the game in his car or some other private place where he could weep, or make dark oaths, or perform whatever other ritualistic sacrifice was required.

We stared after him, blinking in delayed shock.

"Did he just...?"

"Yeah, part of that was definitely from Braveheart."

"No," Matt shook his head in disbelief, gazing towards the parking lot, "did he just walk off the field without giving us the final play?"

...he most certainly did.

The game was tough, but it wasn't finished. A field goal had placed us within striking distance of the win. Just one more touchdown and the night could be ours. If we could just get past their freakin' defense.

"*Unbelievable.*" Matt took off his helmet, hands on his hips. "All right, well, what do you say, Hunt? Twenty seconds left. You got any good ideas?"

"Yeah," I muttered, clutching my fractured ribs. "Send in the alternate."

Ben Goodfellow, an ambitious sophomore who regularly dreamed of ways to kill me for the chance to take my place on the field, paled, and shrank back towards the bench.

The referee screamed something inaudible from the other side of the field and Matt nodded quickly, holding up a finger to ask for one more moment.

"Seriously, man. What's the play?"

"What does it matter?" another player chimed in. "We're on the last down with ninety yards to go. It's over, man. Might as well run out the clock."

Matt shot him a furious look, probably thinking of his post-game 'celebration' with Lauren, but the rest of the team seemed to agree. We had played hard, but were unevenly matched. Sometimes the best thing you could do was throw in the towel and go home.

...or not.

My eyes zeroed in on a solitary figure in the crowd. On a head of dark hair standing unnoticed in the back. There was a pair of hazel eyes staring directly into mine.

For a fleeting moment, the rest of the world seemed to fall away.

"Nate," I said, gesturing the receiver forward, throwing my arm around his shoulder, "if I give you some time...you think you can make it all the way down to the end zone?"

A look of surprise flashed across his face as he glanced towards the far end of the field.

"Ninety yards?" His eyebrows lifted in disbelief before he glanced with sudden concern at my bleeding head wound. "Shit, Jamie, that guy must have hit you really hard."

"Come on, I'm serious—"

"You can't make that throw," Matt interrupted. "No one can make that throw."

The rest of the team was staring. The rest of the stadium was waiting. And somewhere in the crowd, those hazel eyes were still watching my every move.

I slapped the ball into his chest with the hint of a smile.

"Watch me."

With a wild cheer, the team swept back onto the field. Electrified by the crowd. Flushed with that last surge of adrenaline. Clinging to an artificial high—one that was bound to crash and burn when I was inevitably carried away on a stretcher.

Matt seemed to be thinking the same thing.

"Even if you *could* somehow make that throw, how exactly are you going to buy Nate that extra time?" he muttered, forcing a smile as we moved across the grass. "That linebacker's gunning for you, Jamie. Unless you've stashed a Taser in your pads, he's going to break your neck—"

"It's adorable when you worry," I teased. "You should let Lauren see that side of you."

He flashed a reluctant grin, but pulled us to a stop in the center of the field. The Coralto defense was looming up behind him, casting long shadows over the grass. "I'm serious, Jamie. What are you going to do?"

A thrill of fear shot through me as I dared to ask myself the same question. Then my eyes swept the crowd and I backed away with a careless smile.

"I'll improvise."

The players were ready and the field was set. With twenty seconds left on the clock, there was time for one final play. One final touchdown that could tip the score in our favor and take us to the win. We'd just need a small miracle to do it.

I stepped into position and gazed across the row of jerseys to number thirty-seven, the colossus who'd been doing his best to land me in the hospital for the better part of the night.

Even with his helmet down, I could still see the gleam of a smile. The hungry anticipation emanated from his body as he curled his fingers into fists and leaned his body towards mine.

What are you going to do?

Matt's question echoed in my mind, and even though I didn't have an answer I found that I wasn't afraid. Some other feeling had taken over completely. A fierce kind of burning that consumed me from head to toe. Instead of shying away from the pain, I embraced it. Used it. Let it race like liquid fire through my veins. The referee shouted something in the distance and every hair on my body stood on end. My pupils dilated with tunnel vision focus, my mouth went dry.

Then the whistle blew and everything went still.

I'll never be able to accurately explain what happened in that moment. To this day, very little of it makes sense. But at the same time, even as I watched it unfold I knew I could never forget it. I'd remember every second for as long as I lived.

The players on both sides sprang forward at the same time, sending up clouds of debris in their wake. But it was like they were running underwater. Moving at such a glacial speed that I was able to see every bead of sweat. Every distinct blade of grass as they fell to the ground.

Number thirty-seven was charging forward. I saw the tendons tighten in his arms as he barreled through the crowd of jerseys, aiming straight for me.

The ball was in my hand. I don't remember catching it. But even as I gripped the familiar surface beneath my fingers, a single thought kept looping through my mind.

Not yet. Nate needs more time. Don't throw it yet.

Thirty-seven was getting closer. Another second and he'd be right on top of me. My feet dug into the ground, bracing for impact as my eyes zeroed in on his face. One more second—

My hand flew out between us, catching him right in the chest.

Given his size, I expected bones to break. Given his speed, I expected to go flying backwards into the dirt. That's what should have happened. That's what would have made sense.

But there was very little of that fateful game that would end up making sense.

The giant froze in his tracks, all that devastating momentum cut short by my outstretched hand. That strange burn sizzled beneath my skin as I felt the shockwave travel up my arm. Painful, but not debilitating. Not enough to make me flinch. Not enough to make me move.

I felt a sudden intake of breath as he looked down at my hand, unable to understand what was happening, unable to believe it was true. He stared for an endless moment before lifting his eyes to mine. My lips pulled back in a smile.

Then I threw him. With all my might, I threw him backwards into the sea of jerseys still fighting on the line of scrimmage. At the same time, I threw the ball. Aiming for the end zone.

It spiraled right into Nate Jessup's hands.

"TOUCHDOWN!"

I don't know who shouted it first. The entire crowd was on their feet. My hand was still stretched out in front of me, completing the throw, when I was lifted into the air, held high on the shoulders of my screaming teammates as Coralto slunk off the field.

"How did you do that?!" Matt was shouting. "How did you do that?!"

I didn't answer, but he was too excited to care. A second after the final whistle blew, the stands exploded and the crowd raced out onto the field. I tumbled to the ground as we were overrun by a mob of cheering people. A deafening sea of faces painted white and navy blue.

A cloud of streamers burst in my face as I slowly wove my way towards the edge of the field. It was too loud to hear anything. There was too much confetti to see.

It wasn't until she was standing right in front of me that I saw her for the first time.

"Gabby!"

Unlike the rest of the student population, she never attended any sporting events. A part of me was surprised she even knew what time we played. And yet, even as I stood there, I realized that I'd been looking for her in the crowd. I'd been looking for a long time.

"Hey." Those hazel eyes sparkled as she stared up at me with a little grin. "You call that being careful?"

I didn't know what she meant, but an instinctual shiver ran up my spine. My hand cupped over my ear as I leaned towards her, trying to hear over the din of the crowd.

"What?"

She stared at me for a long moment, then shook her head with a grin.

"James Hunt...who knew you had it in you?"

A cloud of confetti swirled in the air around us, catching in her eyelashes, in the dark waves of her hair. Without thinking I reached out and brushed a piece off her cheekbone, my fingers trailing lightly across her skin. Our eyes met, and I dropped my hand.

"I'm glad you came." I bowed my head, feeling suddenly shy. "You know, this morning I was actually going to ask if you—"

"Jamie!"

Before I could finish the sentence I was tackled by no fewer than five guys who were still caught in the throes of the celebration, jumping around with their jerseys hanging round their necks. They tangled together in an ungainly pile, laughing and trying to keep their balance, while I struggled to pull myself free. By the time I did, it was already too late. Gabrielle Tanner was gone.

"He LIVES!" Dave Lipinski caught my hand and held it over our heads. "I thought that Coralto guy was going to bury you alive!"

"Hang on, I just—"

"How did you stop him, anyway?" Another hand grabbed onto my jersey. "I only saw him push past Jeremy and the rest was a blur."

"Just let go for a—"

But it was no use.

The team had swarmed around me and my lovely neighbor was nowhere to be seen. After another second, I abandoned the search altogether and turned to my friends with a silent sigh.

"Forget the linebacker, how the hell did you make that throw?" Nate was flushed and grinning, having received almost as many accolades as me. "That was almost a hundred yards."

"It wouldn't have mattered if you didn't catch it," I replied, starting to smile in spite of myself. My heart was still racing and it was hard not to get carried away. "Nice hands."

"*Nice hands*," Matt scoffed, catching me in a friendly chokehold. "Don't try to be modest, Hunt. Coach Jensen is considering adopting you. He's drawing up the papers as we speak."

There was a chorus of laughter as another burst of confetti shot into the air, blanketing everyone in a sea of navy and white. An automatic cheer rose from the ranks as the cheerleaders joined us, already debating where to carry the celebration on into the night.

"Let's go to my house," I said suddenly, surprising myself just as much as everyone else.

I usually had to be dragged kicking and screaming to those sorts of things. My teammates were usually the ones forcing me along.

They looked up in a moment of shared surprise before letting out a final cheer. This one carried them all the way to the parking lot where they began splitting off into cars, revving the engines and shrieking with laughter as they went tearing down the street on the way to my house.

Matt and I stared after them, standing side by side.

"Your dad's not home, is he?"

"No. He's gone for work."

We lapsed into silence once more, watching the madness unfold.

"Do you even have beer for a party?" he asked with amusement. I bit my lip, considering the dilemma for the first time, and he let out a laugh. "It's cool, we'll pick some up on the way."

Together, we headed over towards the parking lot. Lauren was already waiting beside my jeep. Two more girls whose names I didn't know joined us, and before long we had taken our place in the long line of cars speeding away from the stadium.

The *very* long line of cars.

My heart quickened as I wondered at the wisdom of spontaneously inviting half the student body to my house. Would they even fit? What if my dad somehow found out?

"To the FINALS!" Matt screamed, rolling down his window for effect.

The call was echoed from one car to the next, turning into a wild chant as it lifted into the cool night sky. We burst out laughing and those nervous questions went racing from my mind.

Who cares, right? He told me to have fun, right?

...AND THIS IS WHY I HATE parties.

With the heavy pound of bass throbbing in my ears, I wandered around from room to room. Wondering when it would be over, surveying the general chaos, taking in all the gruesome details as the senior class of Seranto High cheerfully and methodically destroyed my house.

When word had gotten out that Jamie Hunt was throwing a party, it didn't take long for the news to spread. Anyone who had somehow missed the game had ended up at the party. And everyone who'd ended up at the party had decided to bring all their friends.

It was pandemonium, plain and simple. And there was no end in sight.

"Good game, Hunt!"

I glanced over my shoulder to see who had called, but they had already vanished into the crowd. The ground floor of the house had been turned into an impromptu dance hall, and it was hard to make sense of anything amidst the sea of writhing bodies beneath the lights.

"Dude, that was an awesome throw!"

This time, I didn't try to see. With an untouched drink in my hand, I continued my aimless wandering. Flinching every time I heard the sound of shattering glass. Ignoring the stares as best I could. Cringing from the drunken moans coming from inside the hallway closet.

It wasn't until I ducked into the bathroom only to find someone throwing up in the tub that I started drinking. Heavily.

"Jamie!"

I lifted my head as Matt and Lauren stumbled down the hall. He was wearing one of my jackets, and she had a random button stuck in her hair. They clung to each other for balance, grinning drunkenly before falling down beside me on the couch.

"Nice jacket." I lifted my glass with a wry smile. "Thieves go to hell, Matty."

"I didn't steal it," he protested, stretching out his arms to admire the fit. "I found it in the hall closet and decided to liberate it from you. Looks better on me anyway."

I rolled my eyes with a grin, then lowered my glass suddenly as his words clicked. "Wait, that was *you guys* in the..."

My voice trailed off in the wake of their shameless laughter, but before I could push to my feet Matt grabbed me instinctively and pressed another drink into my hand.

"Don't be mad, Jamie. We'll help you clean all this up before your dad comes home, I swear. In the meantime," he waved the drink in my face, "drink this. You'll feel better."

My eyes narrowed and I was about to refuse on principle, when there was another crash from the kitchen and I took the glass with a sigh. "What the heck was I thinking..."

Matt laughed, clapping me on the back as Lauren played with a curl of his hair. "You were thinking that we just won the semi-finals and you wanted to have some fun!"

I watched two juniors tumble into a coatrack, glued together at the mouth and so drunk they actually didn't notice they had fallen. "Yep. Really fun."

Lauren giggled, and leaned across Matt to whisper in my ear. "You just need to unwind a little, Jamie." She tilted her head suggestively to where a cluster of girls was watching me from across the room. The second we locked eyes they started giggling uncontrollably, blushing bright red and speed talking behind their hands. "Just go over there and pick one."

Pick one. Simple as that.

With a tight smile I pushed to my feet, draining my drink in the process. "Yeah, I'll get right on that. I'm getting another drink—you guys want one?"

I glanced down but they were already passionately intertwined, straddling each other on the couch as they threatened to recreate whatever it was they'd started in the hall closet.

And...that's my cue to leave.

"Great game, Jamie!"

"Hunt, awesome party!"

I smiled and waved, weaving my way through the crowd as discreetly as possible before slipping away up the stairs. The upper story was off-limits, as was my father's office. With any luck, I could simply ride out the rest of the party without anyone noticing I was gone—

"Hey!"

My hand flew up to my chest as Alicia ventured out of the upstairs bathroom. One hand was playing absentmindedly with her hair, while the other trailed along the wall for balance. She giggled quietly at my surprise and cocked her head to the darkness behind her.

"Hope you don't mind, I didn't want to wait in line for the other bathroom."

"Of course not."

Unlike most of the people milling about downstairs, Alicia had been to my house plenty of times before. The 'off-limits' rules didn't apply to her.

Unfortunately, she seemed to be thinking the same thing.

"Hiding from your own party, huh?" She leaned into me with a grin, lacing her fingers coyly behind my neck. "Typical Jamie."

My spine stiffened, but I kept a careful smile on my face. As casually as possible I wrapped my hands around hers, trying to coax them loose. She held firm.

"I'm not *hiding*," I countered, "I'm relocating. Big difference."

She laughed again, stretching up onto her toes. "You want me to tell everyone to leave? I can think of some better ways we could fill our time. Just the two of us."

"Aly—"

Her lips pressed against mine, sticky with gloss and clumsy with alcohol. The taste of cheap beer washed over me as I took her gently by the wrists and pulled myself free.

"Come on, hon. Let's go back downstairs."

She resisted, planting her feet with intoxicated stubbornness. "Why are you being so weird this year? We barely spoke all summer and now you're acting like I'm—"

"I'm not acting like anything," I soothed, giving her another quick kiss to stop the argument before it could begin. "But you're drunk, and

I'm exhausted. Let me find you a ride home. We can talk later, okay? I promise."

She stared at me for a moment before her lips curled up into a mischievous smile. "...what if I don't want to talk?"

I let out a genuine laugh, running my fingers through my hair. "You're relentless."

Her eyes twinkled as she skipped to the stairs, glancing back only to give me a little wink. "Count on it."

She disappeared without another word, leaving me standing alone in the dark.

Why can't this night just end?

My eyes closed as I leaned back against the wall, letting the rest of the world fall away as I vanished inside myself. A hundred different images flashed through my mind. Mr. Dixon, gawking at the flaming pencil. Number thirty-seven, staring in shock at my impossibly resilient hand. My father, driving away from me. Me, staring after him from the curb.

And then seeing a face. A beautiful face, smiling up at me from a sea of confetti.

All at once I was on the move, stalking down the hall to my bedroom. It was empty, thank goodness, but I checked twice and carefully locked the door before venturing to the window.

While my house was teeming with a mess of people, the house next door was quiet and dark. I stared at it longingly, safe behind its curtain of trees, when a sudden movement caught my eye. With unnatural focus I took a step closer, face pressed up against the glass.

...what the heck is she doing on the roof?

In hindsight, it was a very stupid thing to do. After all, I'd had a few drinks myself and was feeling a bit unsteady. But that did nothing to stop me from throwing open my window and dropping the two stories, into the dark.

"Shit!"

I landed on my feet then promptly fell over, tumbling into the bushes by the side of my house. A frightened couple gasped and ran for cover, but I didn't think they actually saw who interrupted their tryst. Instead of bothering to find out I silently moved through the shadows, over my front lawn and onto hers, bypassing the walkway this time as I wove through the trees. Never stopping once to think about what I might be doing.

When I got to her front door, I faced an instant dilemma. Knock and risk being turned away or find some other way of getting up to the roof.

I'm pretty sure the alcohol played a major part in the decision.

Five minutes and several choice profanities later, I managed to swing myself up to the second story. It wasn't the easiest climb, but the liquor had numbed me and the darkness cloaked my more pathetic attempts at a graceful entrance. It wasn't long before I was edging my way around the side of the house, just a stone's throw away from—

"HI-YA!"

I doubled over with a cry of pain, slipping precariously towards the edge, when two hands shot out of nowhere and caught me by the sleeve, pulling me safely onto the roof.

"Jamie?!"

Not exactly the suave entrance I was planning.

I lifted my head to see Gabrielle standing in front of me. Breathless and pale. Eyes as wide as saucers. Staring at me with an expression that made me wish I'd fallen after all.

"Uh...hey." I smoothed down my shirt, making a laughable effort to appear sober and nonchalant. "What are you doing here?"

There was a beat of silence.

"What am *I* doing here?" she repeated in disbelief. "I *live* here, Jamie. What the heck are *you* doing on *my* roof?"

That was a good question.

Before I could answer she asked another, correctly interpreting the reason behind my flushed skin and dilated pupils.

"Are you drunk? You climbed up here *drunk*?!"

There wasn't really a way for me to deny it, but that didn't mean a huge part of me didn't want to try. I froze guiltily then shook my head, unable to meet her eyes.

Her lips twitched. She asked again.

"What are you doing here, Jamie?"

Another beat of silence.

"...hiding."

This time, she was unable to hide the smirk.

"You're hiding?" she repeated. Her gaze travelled to the raging party on the other side of the trees before returning to me. "From that?"

That relentless bass line followed her words, and my eyes lifted tentatively to her face.

"Would it be all right if I sat here a while?"

...with you?

Her mouth fell open and she stared at me in shock, not knowing what to say. At first it looked like she was going to refuse, then our eyes met and something changed.

Her smile softened. Then gave me the slightest of nods.

Thanks.

I sat down next to her, dangling my legs over the side of the roof, still trying to act more collected than I was. The night was cooler over here beneath the trees, but not uncomfortable. If anything, it felt good to be in the open air. A little shiver ran across my shoulders as I tilted my head back, gazing silently at the stars.

After a while, she shot me a sideways glance. "So what's going on down there?"

I suppressed a sigh. "A party I'm hosting."

She nodded, paused, and then glanced at me again. "So what are you doing up here?"

This question was far easier to answer, and far more complicated at the same time. I thought about it for a quiet moment before returning her gaze with a shy smile.

"My dad told me to do something fun."

Chapter 5

Gabrielle and I stayed up on the roof for a long time. She never asked me why I had come, and I never asked what she was doing up there in the first place. We sat in a comfortable silence, listening to the wind sweep through the trees, gazing at the moon.

When the party finally started to die down, I pushed to my feet. Most of the booze was out of my system and I was a great deal steadier than when I first arrived.

"Thanks," I said simply.

She glanced over her shoulder, still hugging her knees to her chest. "You're welcome."

And that was it.

I crept back down her roof, ghosted across the sidewalk, and climbed back through my bedroom window. The house was mostly empty, and Matt had apparently left instructions for any and all stragglers to be gone by dawn. So it was with a distracted smile that I fell into bed sometime around four or five in the morning, to fall into a deep and dreamless sleep.

...if only for a little while.

"RISE AND SHINE!"

My curtains pulled back in a single unforgiving gesture, spilling little shards of sunlight all over the room. I flinched with a painful moan, pressing a pillow over my head.

"Out of bed, princess! We've got things to do!"

Matt Harris had always been impossibly cheerful in the mornings. It was an obnoxious quirk that had plagued me ever since making him my best friend in the fourth grade.

"Get out of my house," I mumbled, too disoriented to imagine what reason he possibly had for still being here. "Don't come back. We're broken up."

"Aw, you don't mean that!" He pulled back the blankets the same way as the curtain, leaving me with no protection against the garish light of the outside world. "Come on—*up!*"

My eyes pried open, one at a time, as I forced myself into a sitting position. Quite an admirable effort, I thought, all things considered. Then yesterday's drinking caught up with me in a rush and I swayed unsteadily, fighting back a wave of nausea.

"Seriously, what the hell are you doing here? It's like seven in the morning."

Matt leaned against the doorframe, looking down at me with an amused smile. "It's after ten, and I promised I'd come by in the morning to help you clean up."

...ten? ...in the morning?

I blinked, having a little trouble keeping up.

"Not that we have time for that anymore." Without further ado he began rifling around in my closet, pulling out random pieces of clothing and tossing them to me on the bed. "We have to get moving if we want to make it to the beach."

Beach trip. I completely forgot.

"Yeah, I'm not going to that." I pulled down whatever clothes he'd thrown over my body like a makeshift tent and pressed my forehead into the pillow. "I got my fill of high school spirit last night. I won't be ready for more until after graduation."

The clothes disappeared. Followed immediately by the pillow. At this point, I wouldn't be surprised if he was considering dressing me himself.

"Now I know that can't be true, because you were only at the party for about five minutes," he replied cheerfully, grabbing me by the ankle and pulling me off the bed. I landed on the floor with a painful curse, glaring up at him. "Where did you go, anyway?"

For a split second, I paused. My body tensed of its own accord, and I glanced without thinking at the window that looked out onto the house next door.

"I was in here...sleeping."

We stared at each other for a tense moment, and I suddenly wondered if he knew it wasn't true. But a second later he flashed me a bright smile, bombing me with a pair of shoes.

"You should be all rested up for the beach then."

He vanished without another word, whistling a high-pitched melody as he headed down the stairs—assumedly to wait with increasing impatience in the living room. The only bit of mercy he showed was to leave a steaming latte from the local coffee shop on my dresser, though even that had been strategically placed just out of reach. I'd have to get up if I wanted it.

My pupils dilated automatically as they locked on the paper cup. Maybe if I hooked the edge of the dresser with my foot, I could pull it close enough to—

"JAMIE!"

The dream died as my foot dropped miserably to the floor.

"I'm coming!"

Who doesn't love a day at the beach?

AS IT TURNED OUT, I wasn't the only one having trouble getting up that morning. When Matt and I finally arrived at the shore, loaded up with enough caffeine to make our eyes water, we found that only about half the senior class was already there. Suffering with various degrees of pain.

"I told you," I cursed under my breath, squinting against the punishing sun, "this was a terrible idea. You're officially the only person in the world who doesn't get hangovers."

He clapped me on the back, ignoring the grimace that followed. "All thanks to the power of positivity, my friend. Now come on, I see Lauren."

"You didn't see enough of her in the hallway closet?" I muttered, but I followed him along willingly. Mostly because he had procured yet another cup of coffee on the way to the beach to coax my every step.

Lauren lifted her head weakly as we approached, then lay it back down on the hood of her car. She was stretched out there with several others, looking like some ancient sacrifice the Romans had left out to die. "Jamie...how do we keep letting him do this?" she groaned.

"It's your fault," I said shortly, taking the sunglasses off her head and sliding them over my own face. "I'm not the one having sex with him—you're supposed to control him now."

"He's impossible," she mumbled, dropping her face into her hands.

"And a good morning to you, my love!" Matt replied cheerfully, pressing a kiss to her cheek and a coffee into her hand. I stared after the coffee mournfully, thinking it had been for me. "I see you got my gifts?"

She lifted her head with a glare. "You mean that you baited every rest stop between my house and the beach with caffeine just to get me down here?"

He nodded, looking the lot of us over with a thoughtful frown. "It's actually surprisingly effective. You guys should be careful with that stuff. It's an addiction."

His girlfriend tossed me a pleading look and I nodded solemnly, reaching out to strangle him with my bare hands. He dodged them with a laugh, and proceeded to flip me over into the sand. I lay there, waiting to die, as Lauren fired up the engine and tried to run him over instead.

Then she turned on the radio. Then someone arrived with bagels.

All in all, it was your average beach trip. The lingering effects of the alcohol began to dissipate the higher the sun rose in the sky, and by the time the rest of our bedraggled group deigned to make an appearance we were actually having a fine time.

We watched the girls tan and play volleyball, splashing each other mercilessly in the surf, trying to convince the local burger joint that the beach wasn't too far away for delivery.

"See, this is great right?" Matt stared around the scene like some kind of king, pleased with his efforts at dragging us all out there. "Much better than cleaning up your house."

I glanced over in surprise then dropped my head back with a loud profanity, having already completely forgotten. "You still have to help me do that, this only delays it!"

"I will, I will—relax." He flashed me a teasing grin as some of our other friends plopped onto the sand to join us. "Can't have you hurting that miracle arm of yours before the next game."

There was a spattering of laughter as I dropped my eyes self-consciously to the ground. I hadn't given much thought to what had happened the last night on the field. Chalk it up to massive amounts of alcohol and an over-compartmentalizing mind. But sitting out here, sober in the bright light of day, it was hard not to think about what had happened. It was hard not to replay every inexplicable moment over and over in my head.

"I still don't know how that guy didn't pummel you to death," Matt murmured, doing exactly the same thing. "He was running straight for you."

My hands twitched with a nervous tremor, but I kept it carefully off my face. "Perks of teenage adrenaline. Haven't you heard? We're basically indestructible at this age."

There was another spattering of laughter, and the moment was forgotten. Much like the flaming pencil. Written off as 'one of those things'.

The problem was, I didn't know how many more of 'those things' I was going to get.

"So tell us about Gabrielle Tanner."

My head snapped up in surprise to find a circle of curious eyes staring back at me. The sight of it wreaked havoc on my pulse, and I suddenly wondered if everyone at the beach had seen the two of us sitting together on her roof.

"Why? What do you mean?" I tried to swallow, but my throat was dry. Matt twisted beside me in the sand, interested for the first time as Dave Lipinski repeated the request.

"You guys hooked up for the Gatsby thing, right? How was it?"

Of course! The English project!

"Oh, right." I dropped my eyes to the sand, searching for something innocuous to say. Something that didn't involve food fights and coconut shampoo. "It was fine. She's really smart, you know—so it was quick."

That may have been enough for Dave, but the others wanted dirt. Specifically, the leggy blonde I'd recently jilted cornering me in the upstairs hallway.

"I don't care if she's smart," Alicia snapped, "the girl's a freak." Like most cheerleaders, she was beautiful but mean, petulantly digging her toes into the sand. "Remember when she was the only one to show up for class the day after homecoming? Who in their right mind would just *sit* there?"

My head snapped up and I fixed her with a caustic stare. "So she's a freak because she didn't ditch class like the rest of us? She was probably the only one *not* to get detention, too."

Alicia backed off immediately, surprised by my reaction, and I looked away. I hadn't meant to speak out like that. I hadn't meant to speak out at all. At any rate, it didn't seem to matter. Like hyenas, the rest of them had zeroed in for the kill. Attacking the only person in the senior class who wasn't there to defend herself.

"Jackie saw her snorting a line of coke in the girls' locker room last year."

"Yeah, and you know she *totally* had a fling with Mr. Henson."

"That's probably why her parents are never around. They don't want to be around her any more than the rest of us..."

On and on it went, circling around the happy little beach. The assassination of one girl's character as sport for the masses. Growing more and more vicious as it picked up speed.

Once or twice, I opened my mouth to stop it. Once or twice, I considered getting up and just walking away. But I could think of no plausible explanation for doing so. Finally, after a few minutes I shot Matt a sideways glance, cocking my head towards the bloodbath.

"Do something."

He was the only one who hadn't participated, though he'd been watching me carefully ever since I shot Alicia down. His eyebrows lifted when I made the request and, despite my best effort to look normal, a very peculiar expression shadowed across his face.

"Why? Why do you care, Jamie?"

There it was—right in front of me. A question so direct that there was no way to ignore it or deflect it. His eyes pierced me as I floundered a moment, trying to think of what to say. Then another burst of laughter rang up from the oblivious crowd and I bowed my head.

"I don't," I answered quietly. "I don't care."

Chapter 6

Gabrielle and I didn't say another word to each other for the rest of the week.

It wasn't her fault, though it *was* mine. Ever since that day at the beach, I couldn't shake the feeling that I was standing on the edge of something. A precipice I never knew was there. The morning that we returned to school, she'd tried coming up to me in the hall. Sitting in the back of our history class, she'd leaned forward to catch my eye. But I carefully avoided her each time, and by seventh period she'd stopped trying. From that day forth, food fights and secret smiles were forgotten—everything went back to the way it had been before.

It didn't start that day at the beach. It started the night of the party. It started on her roof.

The thought unsettled me as I picked up my backpack and started walking distractedly towards the men's locker room after school. It was a balmy Thursday afternoon. The kind that harkened nostalgically back to the days of summer, fiercely resisting the chillier hands of fall.

Why did I even go up there? I asked myself for the hundredth time. *A million ways to escape that party, and I had to go climbing onto Gabrielle Tanner's roof.*

The pep squad had cheerfully, repeatedly, vandalized our lockers after the big game. A bunch of standard stuff, for the most part. Balloons, exploding dye packs, a plate of macaroons that went unnoticed for two days and attracted several colonies of ants. But on this particular day, someone had gotten a little creative with mine. The second I pulled it open, a literal mountain of pictures tumbled down on me. They were pictures of random women, baring their breasts.

"What the—?"

I gasped, staring at the floor around me, blushing to high heaven when I saw what was staring back. For a split second, I was too stunned to move. Then someone catcalled behind me and I dropped down to my knees, scrambling to pick them all up.

"Jamie Hunt." Matt sauntered up with a grin, shaking his head with mock disapproval as he watched my frantic effort. "I applaud the charisma...but do it on your own time."

I shot him a murderous glare, gathering up the pictures as quickly as I could. "Did you do this?"

"Did *I* do this?" He let it hang for a moment, then shook his head. "No. But will I take one for later?" After quick consideration, he plucked a busty brunette from my hand. "*Absolutely.*"

I smacked him in the kneecaps, failing to see the humor. "Could you stop laughing and help me with this? It's only a matter of time be-fore—"

"Hunt?"

The two of us froze, and then looked up slowly to see Coach Jensen standing just a few feet away. Arms folded and a slightly bewildered expression on his face.

Great...this is just great.

Things had been awkward with my coach ever since he'd given me a hand-written letter of gratitude, along with copy of Great Expectations—for reasons that remained unclear.

My pulse faltered as my skin paled about twenty shades. "Coach, I can explain—"

He held up a hand to stop me, closing his eyes with the infinite patience of a Buddhist monk. "Whatever gets you through the game, son."

Without another word he swept out the door and onto the field, leaving my best friend and me kneeling in a pile of erotica on the locker room floor. We froze for a minute, and then turned to each other at the same time.

"That was—"

"Yeah, let's *never* talk about that again."

With a sense of renewed urgency, we got to work picking up the photos. It wasn't an easy task. There had to be over a thousand scattered around the floor, and the rest of the team was quick to get in on the fun—gawking, and hollering, and generally laughing their asses off.

I tolerated it as best I could, even rolling my eyes with a grin as some of them began dancing the pictures around, but I should have known the worst was yet to come.

The main door banged open and everyone fell silent at once—staring in open-mouthed shock as angry footsteps echoed over the tile. The hair on the back of my neck stood on end, and the roof of my mouth went bone dry.

I knew who it was before I saw her. I could smell the coconut shampoo.

"...this can't be happening."

Sure enough, a moment later Gabrielle Tanner stormed around the corner. Flashing eyes, curled fists, and the kind of feminine rage that made men dive for cover. She'd clearly been steeling herself for the confrontation for the last several minutes, but stopped dead in her tracks when she saw the cluster of naked women peeking out from my hands.

It was worse than I could have ever imagined. Her lips parted in sheer astonishment, and I silently begged the gods to show some mercy and kill me on the spot. There was an excruciating moment where neither one of us said a word. Then she looked me square in the eyes.

"Sorry...didn't mean to interrupt your pre-game ritual."

My eyes snapped shut as whatever dignity I had left went racing out the window. Even my fellow teammates had the good sense to shrink out of sight and keep silent. Only my insufferable best friend seemed to think it was the appropriate time for him to speak.

"It's not a game, Tanner." Matt stopped pretending not to be eavesdropping long enough to correct her on this one trivial thing. "It's a practice."

I shot him a look of furious disbelief before turning back to her. "More importantly, I'm not—"

She raised her hands, much the same way that my coach had just moments before. "No judgment here."

"Yeah, but this isn't—"

"Look," she interrupted dryly, "I couldn't care less how you and the rest of these jackals choose to spend their time. I'm here because our project is due this Monday, and since you spontaneously decided not to speak to me we haven't been able to set up a time to meet."

The words burned, but she had every right to say them. I dropped my head in shame, feeling somehow more embarrassed than I had at any point since opening my locker.

"Yeah," I began quietly, "about that—"

"I don't care," she said, devoid of emotion, looking as though she hadn't given the whole thing more than a few seconds' thought. "Just pick a time so I can get out of here. Saturday? Sunday?"

"Can we do it tomorrow?" I asked suddenly. In my periphery I saw Matt shoot me a look, but I kept my eyes on Gabby, repeating the question. "Can you come over tomorrow?"

She looked a little surprised at the sudden insistence in my voice, but showed no other emotion than that. A second later she shrugged, and began walking away.

"If you like."

I let out a tortured sigh the second she was out of sight, having now lived the classic high school nightmare. It was a feeling that only intensified when she doubled back a second later.

"By the way, if you're looking for a sure thing I'd go with the redhead." She flicked one of the pictures in my hands. "Don't waste a tissue on the blonde..."

And with that, my mortification was complete.

When she left this time, it was to the cheering applause of the entire football team. Nate Jessup even held the door open and saluted as she sailed by. Only Matt managed to keep it together, patting my back as I stared after her, looking like I'd swallowed a bug.

"Hey man...it could have been worse."

I kept my eyes on the door, too demoralized to move. "How?"

He thought about it, winced sympathetically, then offered an optimistic take. "You could have been *in* the pictures."

NEEDLESS TO SAY, I was a little distracted by the time we finally made it out onto the field to practice. The final game wasn't until the following Friday, but that didn't mean our coach wasn't already having his traditional coronary—screaming out commands as he paced back and forth on the sidelines, taking solace only in the promise of my miraculous new arm.

"IF YOU THINK THAT'S GONNA CUT IT AGAINST MARIPOSA, YOU'VE LOST YOUR FLIPPIN' MINDS! I WANT TO SEE SOME BLOOD OUT THERE! RUN IT AGAIN!"

Matt slid to a stop beside me, taking off his helmet and squinting into the sun. "Glad to see his blood pressure medication isn't interfering with these precious moments."

I started to smile and then pointedly ignored him instead, still smarting from his unwanted participation during the whole locker room debacle. He shoved me with a playful grin and trotted back to the line of scrimmage, leaving me alone with my thoughts.

Tomorrow. She's coming over tomorrow.

I tried not to overanalyze it. Tried not to ask myself why I'd insisted she come over on that specific day. The project was due on Monday, right? It made sense to hurry.

"Hunt! Wake up and throw the ball!"

With robotic precision, I lifted my arm and let loose a perfect spiral—throwing it farther and farther as the receivers went through their paces running down the field.

Yeah, but...tomorrow?

Another series of hard throws as I tuned out the nagging voice in my head, focusing on the rest of the tragic encounter instead.

What did she think of me?

All jokes aside, I honestly couldn't tell. The mind of the high school girl was hard enough to decipher, and Gabrielle Tanner was more complicated than most. She...tolerated me. Our time on the roof at least proved that much. There was even the slightest chance that she might have enjoyed my company. But I could just as easily have been wrong. She certainly didn't look like she enjoyed my company today. Although I'm sure she certainly got a good laugh out of it.

Why did I care what she thought of me?

This one was even harder to answer. I could always go the easy route—cling to the comfort of clichés. She was an attractive girl who lived next door, and I was a teenage guy who wasn't blind. Of course some part of me wondered what she was thinking. But if I was being honest, it was something more than that.

There was a reason I'd invited her over tomorrow. There was a reason I'd climbed up onto that roof.

"Hunt! Throw to Jessup! Watch the sides!"

I pulled my arm back again in that same introspective stupor. Too caught up to see what was going on around me. Too distracted to notice the white van pulling onto the curb.

My head was miles away...until I heard the scream.

At first, I didn't understand what was going on. The scene, while simple enough, was utterly incomprehensible. Twelve men in bulletproof vests were advancing on one terrified teenager.

It wasn't real life. It was something I'd see on the news. What was something like that doing at my school? Was this some kind of joke? Then I recognized the teenager.

...Nate?

He was frozen like a caged animal, paling to the exact same color as the vans. He slowly raised his hands, and even from a great distance I could see he was shaking from head to toe.

"Please, I..." He didn't seem to know how to finish that sentence, but he was asking all the same. "Please..."

A car door slammed and I jumped out of my skin. A radio crackled with static. Even more men with military-grade weapons swept onto the field. Little red dots were dancing around on his grass-stained jersey. Orbiting in dangerous circles just over his heart.

...this can't be real...

I couldn't believe it. Couldn't begin to process what was going on. I glanced at my coach, too stunned to speak. *Do something. Say something.* But my coach just stood there. Same as me.

"Nathaniel Jessup?"

It was impossible to tell which of the men had spoken. Under their helmets and armor, they all looked the same. But Nate cringed the second he heard it, looking as though he'd never heard anything more terrifying than the sound of his own name.

"There-there's been a mistake. I'm not..." He glanced back at the rest of us, frozen perfectly still where we'd been standing. "Just give me a second to explain."

But that brief acknowledgment was proof enough.

There was another crackle of static as one of the men lifted a radio to his lips. "He's here on the football field. Number twenty-four. All clear for extraction."

"NO!"

The ball lay forgotten on the grass beside him. Men in suits were closing in on every side.

"Wait!" he cried, throwing up his hands as he backed away. "I swear I'll never use it! On my mother's life—I *swear*! Just-just please don't do this!"

He tripped over the football in a panicked retreat, just a few feet away from where he'd caught it and led the school to a glorious victory less than a week before.

"Coach!" he called out desperately, too frightened to turn around. "Tell them that I won't use it! Tell them—"

An electric blast shot out of one of the guns, dropping Nate where he stood.

"We got him contained."

The radio came down and the men surged forward, closing around Nate's body with the grim efficiency of those who had done it many times before. After checking to make sure he still had a pulse, they loaded him into one of the vans. Leaving only the faintest imprint in the grass.

I hadn't moved an inch since it happened. The whole thing was over just seconds after it had begun. Then one of the men in the helmets recognized me and gave me the slightest of nods.

I barely made it to the parking lot before I threw up in front of my car.

Chapter 7

I walked home instead. I didn't trust myself to drive right then.

Practice had been unofficially canceled after our star receiver had been cable-tied in the back of a van, and the rest of the team dispersed without saying a word. I had no idea if anyone even went back to their lockers. I changed and just left.

It was a ten-minute walk, but I did it in five. Moving briskly, with my hands pressed deep in my pockets. Nate's words replaying in my head over and over again on an endless loop. The second I made it through the door I locked it behind me, falling back against it as my eyes watered and fixed on the wall.

There's been a mistake, I'm not...

The bag slipped off my shoulder, dropping with a thud on the floor.

I swear I'll never use it! On my mother's life—I swear!

I slid down to the marble tile, hugging my knees to my chest.

Please don't do this!

My eyes snapped shut and I was momentarily grateful no one was there to see me cry.

He swore on his mother's life. That was ironic.

They'd be coming for her next, if they hadn't gotten her already. If they knew about him, then they surely knew about her as well. Recovery would already be underway.

I sucked in a breath, pressing my forehead to my knees.

That's what they called it...*recovery*.

Like the gifts of the supernatural were something the government had simply misplaced, and needed to return to its rightful location. Like they were setting something right, rectifying a geographical mistake, rather than claiming something that had never been theirs to begin with.

A chill swept over my skin, and I mentally checked myself.

The *abilities* of the supernatural. We weren't allowed to call them gifts.

A blurry image of the football field swam before my eyes, and I wished I could claw the memory from my head. In a million different scenarios, I saw myself rushing forward. In a million bloodshot hypotheticals, I saw myself being a better man.

But even if I tried...what was the point?

It was against the law—what Nate was. It was against the law to possess that kind of power. Even if it wasn't his fault. Even if he was still Nate— the guy I'd spent countless hours with on the football field.

It was only seven o'clock when I climbed into bed that night, feeling shaken and cold. I pulled the covers up to my chin like a child, shivering as the trees next door cast long shadows over my wall. Hoping very much that I wouldn't dream. Trying not to imagine all those people sitting down to watch the evening news...

THE STRANGEST THING happened the next morning: the sun came up. Just like it always did. Just like nothing had happened. I stared at it without blinking, ignoring the pulsing screech of my alarm, then finally shaking off the covers and swinging my feet onto the floor.

I swear I'll never use it! On my mother's life—I swear!

No matter how much time passed, I couldn't get his voice out of my head.

I didn't think I ever would.

The morning routine was dull and lifeless. I put no thought into the actions and started walking downstairs three times before remembering I wasn't wearing a shirt. My appetite had vanished around the same time electric charges were shot into my friend, and I bypassed the kitchen entirely before heading into the garage...and remembering I'd left my car at the school.

That's when I began the slow walk to school.

Call it morbid curiosity or masochistic whim, but I walked around the length of the campus before heading inside. Pausing a moment on the edge of the football field, right where Nathanial Jessup had made his final stand. The bell rang, but I barely heard it—staring with vacant eyes as I knelt to examine the grass.

No scorch marks or other indication of a struggle. The groundskeeper had come by and cut it last night for good measure, leaving the whole field a uniform two inches tall.

"Jamie?"

I leapt to my feet with a start, trying to control my frantic pulse. Gabby had moved so quietly that I hadn't heard her approach until she was standing right next to me, staring down at the same spot in the grass.

"It's weird, right?" she mused, wrapping her arms around her chest. "Almost like it didn't even happen."

I'd been thinking the same thing, but simply nodded in reply. Keeping my fists buried in my pockets and my eyes fixed on the field. I could still hear echoes of those screams. Echoes I knew would haunt me for years to come.

She studied me for a moment, brow tightening in concern, then reached ever so tentatively for my arm. "Are you okay?"

I flinched from her touch without thinking, flushing guiltily at the same time. "Of course. Why?"

The words fired out like bullets. Too direct. Too quick. She paused before answering.

"I just meant...you were here when it happened, right? Must have been tough."

Must have been tough. She was trying to be sweet.

My lips parted with a scripted reply, but it died on my lips the longer I looked at the grass. Instead I found myself mimicking her gesture, wrapping my arms protectively over my chest. "It was tough."

We stood there for a while in silence, long after the rest of the students had vanished inside for class. Long enough for the sprinklers to come on, soaking the field clean.

Like it never even happened. Right.

"Come on," she urged, finally breaking the silence. Then, in a surprising move, she linked her arm through mine, leading me towards the school. "Let's get to class."

IT'S UTTERLY AMAZING, the lengths the human brain will stretch to minimize cognitive dissonance and prevent itself from harm.

First period, the only thing anyone could talk about was Nate. By lunchtime they'd moved away from specifics, and were discussing the broader generalities of the purge. When afternoon classes rolled around, his English partner was reassigned and people started making weekend plans. By the end of the day, Coach Jensen had filled the vacancy on the team.

I was not immune. In fact, I was more eager to move on than the rest.

"So...Tanner's coming over today, huh?"

Matt and I were headed to the parking lot after the final bell, playing mischievously with our keys, locking and unlocking our cars to make the people standing closest jump back and glare. My eyes flashed up at his question but I kept a carefully neutral face, trying to act like I hadn't been thinking about it every second since lunch.

"Why do you always call her by her last name?" I countered. "We've known her since kindergarten—why can't you call her Gabby?"

"Because Gabrielle Tanner's not really a *first name* kind of girl." He pressed the panic button and smirked as the freshmen walking past his Ferrari yelped and scattered. "She's more of a...*sucks to be trapped as her*

English partner kind of girl." He tossed the keys from hand to hand, giving me a curious stare. "Which again begs the question: Why today?"

Why did a guy who'd spent the majority of the summer lobbying Doritos to rebrand his favorite flavor of chips have to be so damn perceptive the other ten percent of the time?

I shrugged, trying to run out the clock as I picked up the pace to my car. When it became clear that wasn't going to work I offered a half-hearted, "It's due Monday. Gotta finish it up."

He stared at me for another moment and then let it go, clapping me on the back as we went our separate ways. "At least the project itself isn't so bad."

My lips quirked up in a smile as I muttered under my breath, "At least you got to be Gatsby..."

It wasn't until I was halfway home that the nerves kicked in and the reality of my little study date hit me for the first time. Gabrielle was coming over to my house. Usually, that wouldn't be a problem. But this was the 'dad's been away' version of my house. The kind with bags of recycling tossed in the corner, and Chinese delivery cartons stacked on the floor. Unless I was mistaken, a lamp that had gotten broken at the party was still in the downstairs bathroom.

I stepped on the gas.

Thirty minutes later, I had cleaned and showered. The house was immaculate, the bins of trash and recycling were neatly stacked out front, and I was just sweeping up the last of the glass when there was a sudden knock on the door.

A wave of anxiety swept over me and I froze where I stood, staring comically between the dustpan in my hand and the front door. In the end I stashed the pan in the hallway closet and jogged quickly down the hall to open it, pausing only a moment to smooth my messy hair.

"Hey," I tried to act as casual as she'd been at her house, pulling open the door with a welcoming smile, "right on time."

She cocked her head with a frown. "Did we set up a time?"

The smile faltered, but I kept it plastered on my face. "No...I guess we didn't." *Recover, dude! Recover!* "Come on in."

I stepped back to allow her inside but she stayed right where she was, folding her arms as her smile morphed into a kittenish glare.

"First we need to straighten some things out. You've been a total ass to me, Hunt."

Wow—direct. And completely negating recent events.

My own smile sharpened as my fingers dug into the door. "Oh, I think we're even."

She raised her eyebrows, and looked completely surprised to be challenged. "You completely ignored me for the better part of the week—"

"—then you humiliated me in the men's locker room." She opened her mouth to argue, and I quickly added, "in front of the entire football team. With *porn*."

There suddenly wasn't a doubt in my mind that it was her. Not a single doubt. This girl had been snubbed, derided, and ignored by the entire student population for the better part of four years. She was used to it from everyone else but, for whatever reason, she wasn't tolerating it from me. Instead, she'd forced herself to be seen. Instead, she'd demanded retribution.

It was a momentary standoff, then her lips twitched up with a grin. "Fine. We're even."

To make things official, she even offered a reconciliatory hand. I rolled my eyes at the mock formality but shook hands anyway, taking advantage of the opportunity to pull her inside. She stumbled onto the tile with a grin, then froze.

Here we go...moment of truth.

It never failed. Every time someone new came to my house, they stopped a moment in the entryway. Staring up at the high ceilings. Glancing at the pictures on the walls. Stifling an automatic shiver as they imagined the man who lived upstairs.

My father...not me.

To say that Alexander Hunt had achieved international fame would be downplaying it to a massive degree. He'd been knighted in England. Praised by the pope in Rome. The Secretaries of both Defense and State had both been regular fixtures at our house for dinner. The Supreme Allied Commander of NATO once attended my little-league baseball game.

But such acclaim was built on a framework of fear and notoriety. If one in every five hundred people had been born with supernatural abilities, that left a lot of friends, family, peers, and cohorts with a personal grudge against dear ol' dad.

Our house had been firebombed when I was ten years old. When I was twelve, a woman with flaming hands had tried to kidnap me from a theater program after school. It wasn't easy growing up with such a recognizable family name, but therein lay the beauty of Seranto, California. Perhaps the only paternal decision my father ever made was to move us from Manhattan to the tiny seaside town. A town with fewer than three thousand people. A town where every privileged person in every gated house was going to watch me grow up and keep close watch on everything I did.

The name ceased to have any meaning. I was no longer James Hunt, son of the world-renowned commandant. I was Jamie. The kid who lived on Tressmen Street. The kid who'd gone to daycare and then on to elementary school, then high school with all the rest. I'd performed in enough school plays and tone-deaf talent shows to cease to have any novelty.

Now, the only time I ever felt the difference between me and the rest of the world was when someone new stepped into my house.

"You okay?" I asked in a cursory tone.

I hated it. Absolutely *hated* the thrill of excitement and fear that shot up my spine the second they cleared the front door. Most days, I would have cut off my own leg to have a normal house.

Today, I would have cut off more than that.

"Yeah." Gabrielle quickly averted her eyes, fiddling uncomfortably with the strap on her bag. "I've just...never been in here before."

That was a gracious save. One this household probably didn't deserve.

"You want something to drink?" I changed the subject quickly. "We've got..." To be honest, I didn't know what we had. I usually stuck to coffee or water and nothing else. "...stuff."

She flashed me a hopeful smile. "Does that include coffee?"

Ahh... now that's a girl after my own heart.

"Yeah," I replied, cocking my head towards the kitchen, and gestured her forward, "right in here."

She followed me closely without seeming to be aware of it herself. Fingers gripped tight on her bag, muscles tensed to spring. I watched with secret sympathy, reading the telltale signs.

"Nice to have the house to ourselves, huh?" I gestured casually about the kitchen, pouring ground coffee into the filter on the machine. "Everything's easier without parents."

He's not here, Gabby. No need to be nervous.

Her eyes flashed up, worried she'd offended me, and then she saw my expression and brightened with a sudden smile. "Jamie Hunt, you're a lot smarter than I gave you credit for."

My hand jerked, spilling coffee all over the counter. "Umm...thanks?"

She laughed quietly, grabbing a paper towel off the rack to clean up the spill. "It's a compliment. Usually people who look like you turn out to be a complete waste of time."

My eyebrows lifted as she flushed an incriminating shade of red. "People who look like me?"

There was a beat.

"You actually have to *turn on* the coffee maker."

I dropped my eyes quickly to the complicated machine, punching in the correct sequence of buttons to start the magic brew. Once it got going I innocently herded her towards the living room, fighting a smile the whole time. "After you."

"Shut up, Jamie."

Without further conflict, we settled onto the couch to work. Carefully avoiding each other's eyes, while being hyperaware of each other the entire time. It was exactly like it had been at her house, only this time we'd done it once before. We'd had a week to overanalyze all those micro-expressions and gestures. We'd spent a night silently star-gazing on the roof.

"Is your house always this cold?"

My head snapped up with a start. She was hugging a pillow to her chest. Legs tucked under her. Her fingers were trembling as they curled into her long sleeves.

"Sorry," I said quickly, jumping to my feet to change the thermostat, "my dad likes to keep it this way. I don't even notice it anymore..."

She watched my every move. Weighing each word with a metric I didn't understand.

"And he's out?" she asked lightly.

My fingers paused over the controls before I cast a reassuring glance over my shoulder. "Yeah. Won't be back until Monday."

She stared a second longer then visibly relaxed, releasing her death grip on the pillow as the frigid air was replaced with a gust of heat. "How are you coming along with Daisy?"

I blinked, trying desperately to place the name. "Sorry?"

She glanced down at her paper, stifling another smile. "The letters. Did you write the ones from Daisy yet?"

Of course, the damn project. Keep up, Jamie.

"Oh, uh...yeah." I rifled around in my bag, setting them in a neat stack on the sofa between us. "She's a little temperamental—not gonna lie."

Gabrielle's head jerked up, then she snatched the top paper off the pile. "Yeah? Well, the Gatsby I'm writing is unbearably full of himself."

Our eyes met, twinkling with the same smile.

"I'll bet he's charming."

"He's really not."

We stared for a moment, then looked away at the same time. Each of us pretending to read each other's papers. Each pretending not to notice the other, sitting just inches away.

"Are you hungry?" I asked suddenly, without any kind of plan. She had provided food at her house. The least I could do was provide the same. "I could make something..."

Really? You suddenly know how to cook?

She stared at me in surprise before pushing to her feet. "Yeah, okay."

...shit.

I flashed a casual smile as we headed back to the kitchen, trying not to act as 'unbearably full of myself' as her letters would lead me to believe. In what I thought was a brilliant start, I poured us both a glass of orange juice. Then I opened an empty cupboard and realized that I'd made a huge mistake. *Make* something! What the heck is there to *make*?

"Thanks." She took the glass with a thoughtful smile. "That's sweet. You've always been sweet," she added, like she was realizing it for the first time, "ever since you had that crush." A sudden smile lit her face. "At least, you used to be—until you left me for Miss Calvenetti."

I spat out a mouthful of orange juice, disgraced beyond repair. "How did you know about that?"

She let out a pretty laugh and perched on the counter, tossing back a curtain of soft chocolate hair. "All the girls knew. That was the year you boys left us to go hang out in the science room at lunch. Every day for a full semester—that's dedication. Especially considering the room smelled like formaldehyde."

I absorbed this for a moment, and then bowed my head with a blush. "I meant...how did you know I had a crush?"

"You gave me your Lunchable once, when I forgot my food at home." She took a swig of orange juice, swinging her legs on the counter. "Lunchables are hot currency in the fifth grade."

Try as I might, I could think of nothing to say to this. In the end I simply smiled, discreetly checking cabinet after cabinet as I looked for something to cook.

It was a highly embarrassing venture. While I didn't have any way to know for sure, I imagined that most people's kitchens were stocked with, well, food. Not the endless supply of frozen dinners and microwavable entrees designed for people who chronically ate alone.

"Sorry," I mumbled with a flush, "it's usually just me." Without daring to meet her eyes, I pulled my phone hopefully from my pocket. "You want another pizza? If I promise to behave?"

A strange expression lit her face and she nodded slowly, watching as I pressed a number on speed-dial and recited a credit card number by memory before ending the call.

"Hawaiian?" she asked in surprise. "I thought it was terrible."

I glanced at her quickly, then shrugged it off. "It's not so bad."

A sudden silence descended on the room, one that threatened to unlock all those things we'd been trying not to say. I quickly pushed away from the counter, returning to the sofa without another backward glance. She followed curiously behind me, looking around all the while.

"So you're on your own most of the time, huh?"

I turned around to see her looking at a picture mounted on the wall. It was one of me, my mom, and my dad on my fourth birthday. We were all in matching clothing, awkwardly posed.

"Yeah," I said briskly, staring at the first sentence on her paper without taking in a single word. "My dad...travels a lot."

She shot me a quick look before returning her eyes to the picture. "I'll bet." It was quiet for a moment, then she glanced at me again. "That's your mom?"

My face warmed, then saddened at the same time. "Yeah."

"She's beautiful."

A sharp pain tightened my chest and I returned my gaze to the paper. "Yeah, she was."

Unlike most of the kids at Seranto High, I'd grown up in a one-parent household. My mother had been killed in a traffic pile-up when I was four. I was too young for many memories, mostly just fleeting emotions and an abstract sense of loss. When I was a kid, I often pretended to remember more than I did. Trying to make myself believe it was true.

"And your dad...you never feel bad about what he does?"

There was a hitch in my breathing, but I kept my eyes on the page. Few people had ever been bold enough to ask the question.

Of course it had to be Gabrielle Tanner.

I shifted uncomfortably, pretending not to feel her probing stare.

In all honesty, I tried not to think about it all that much. As much as it might impact the rest of the world, my father's profession had little to do with me. I claim to have grown up in a one-parent household, but more often than not the only person living there was me.

When he was home, he locked himself away in his study. When he was away, he never checked in or called. Five years ago, he'd been named 'commandant' in a private ceremony at the White House. I'd been surfing with my friends in Cabo and failed to attend.

We were family, but not family at the same time. Two people living utterly separate lives.

"A little, sure," I finally replied, staring blindly at the paper. "But what's the alternative?"

Her eyebrows lifted slowly as she sank beside me on the couch.

"What's the alternative?" she repeated.

Why does she have to make me say it? I feel like an asshole every time I do.

"You've seen the news, you know the statistics on unchecked abilities." The words were no longer my own. I was repeating the party line. "Nine times out of ten they end up hurting someone, and that person usually isn't themselves. It's not a random act of injustice. They need to be isolated—for their protection and for ours."

She nodded casually. Only someone sitting very close could see the way her fingernails dug into her palms. I was sitting very close. "Do you think Nate was dangerous?"

It hit me like a blow to the stomach. Just one simple question and I was right back on that football field, listening to the terrified screams of my friend.

"Nate..." I trailed off, bowing my head.

Since I woke up that morning, *all* I wanted to do was talk about Nate. Even when I tried to change the subject to something else. It was still there even when I worked so hard to erase the images from my mind.

But now that we were finally talking, it seemed there was nothing left to say.

"I don't think it's his fault," I answered quietly. "I don't think he had a choice."

She stared at me for a long moment as every hint of emotion drained from her face. By the time she looked away, it was like she was a different person. Someone I didn't know. "...he sure doesn't now."

That was the end of whatever might have been starting between me and Gabrielle Tanner at the study session. We worked in silence for the remainder of the hour, not even speaking when the pizza arrived and I got up to get plates. I briefly considered making some kind of joke about ranch dressing. I'd even located a bottle and placed it front and center in the fridge.

But all that was behind us now.

We finished just a little while later and I stood there awkwardly as she gathered up her things. It was the last time we'd have any official reason to speak with one another, and a sense of quiet urgency came over me as she headed to the door.

"Can I walk you home?"

She glanced back in surprise, one hand already on the door. "...what?"

I blushed, but held her gaze—repeating the question in a quiet voice. "Can I walk you home?"

Her eyes flashed outside before returning incredulously to my face. "Jamie, it's like thirty seconds away—"

"I know."

She stared at me for another moment, using that same confusing metric before rolling her eyes with a sigh. "All right."

I was careful not to smile as I grabbed my coat, opening the door before she could touch it and holding it graciously as she walked outside. The temperature had dropped with a sharp chill, the kind where you're almost able to see your breath. I took one look at her bare arms, and instead of putting the coat myself I draped it over her shoulders.

She startled, but didn't look at me. Faltered, but didn't slow her pace.

Exactly thirty seconds later, we were standing in front of her door. It had gotten even colder the second we walked into the cover of the trees and I was the one shivering now. My hands dug deep into my pockets as an icy wind swept over my arms.

"Well...goodnight." I turned around to leave, when her hand shot out and caught my arm.

"I have another question."

My eyes shot warily to her face, and I suddenly wished I'd stayed inside. "I'm pretty sure you used all of those up."

"It's my last one, I promise." Her eyes sparkled in the dusky twilight, catching the light of the first evening stars. "Why did you ask me to come over?"

My back stiffened and I quickly pretended not to have understood. "Our project's due Monday—"

"Why today?" she pressed, staring up at me curiously. "Why did you insist on today?"

She really was beautiful. That face, those eyes. A part of me felt like I could stare forever into those eyes. Spend an eternity of twilights trying to coax that sparkling smile.

But I would never get the chance.

My shoulders slumped as I stepped back, off the porch. I tried to play it off, but the skill was beyond me. In the end, I simply shrugged. Backing into the dark with a sad smile.

"Because it's my birthday."

Chapter 8

What the heck's wrong with me?!

I fled the Tanners' house and raced back to mine at a speed that bordered on panic, letting out a vile curse the second I pushed through the door. It slammed shut behind me, and for the second time in two days I found myself falling back against it, covering my face with my hands.

What the hell was I thinking?

I hadn't planned on saying anything. I didn't even know what infernal spirit had inspired me to walk her home. But suddenly, there I was. Standing on Gabrielle Tanner's front porch.

"Damnit!"

I cursed again, banging my head into the door.

What was I talking about—I knew what spirit! The same one that had possessed me to climb onto her roof a week earlier. And probably the same one that had made me double back to the local convenience store just to pick up a bottle of ranch. Probably the same one who thought it would be funny if I offered to cook dinner! And all the while, I *should* be thinking about—

"James?"

I jerked back with a gasp, clutching at my chest. A second later, a tall man walked out of the living room and I became hyperaware of the fact that I'd been screaming profanities at the top of my lungs.

"Dad!" I stepped forward in surprise, peeling myself off the door. "What are you doing here? I thought you weren't coming back until Monday."

"Plans changed," he replied simply, looking me up and down. "But it sounds like you've been having a more interesting night than me. Where were you, James?"

Everyone else called me Jamie. I didn't know why he always insisted on calling me James.

My face blanched, but I tried my best to play it off. Not the easiest thing to do with echoes of my enraged obscenities still ringing throughout the house.

"I was just...out for a walk."

How ironic for the renowned inquisitor to have such a transparent son.

His lips twitched, but even though he saw through the lie in a second he didn't care enough to pursue it further. What trouble could I possibly get up to on Tressmen Street?

"Well, at any rate, it's good to see you." He gestured me forward, and after a few false starts the two of us succeeded in a stiff, one-armed hug. "How was your game?"

I was surprised that he was asking, but the game couldn't matter less. Not today.

Are you serious? Do you really not remember?

"It was good. We won."

My eyes stared into his. Silently pleading.

Come on, Dad. You have to remember.

"That's great, kid." He clapped me on the shoulder. "I wish I could have seen it. I had to move some mountains just to make it back tonight."

A surge of relief warmed me through and through.

"Do you..." I took a step closer, a tentative smile lighting up my face. "Do you want to go out for dinner or something?"

His phone buzzed and he glanced down distractedly, punching in a few numbers before slipping it back into his coat. "I just got home, James. Why would I want to go out for dinner?"

Like popping a balloon, that relief disappeared. Leaving me empty and cold.

Yep. He totally forgot.

"Forget it...no reason."

I took a step back, watching with a blank stare as he took off his coat and began emptying his pockets onto the credenza. He must have pulled into the driveway just as Gabrielle and I had vanished into the trees. Otherwise, there was no way I could have missed him.

There was another violent buzzing from one of the phones and I started backing towards the stairs, flashing a tight smile as he raised his hand in an apologetic wave.

Since I was five years old, those phones were my cue to leave.

"This is Hunt—"

I tuned out the conversation and headed up to my room, trying not to appear as dejected as I felt. It was a childish reaction I knew, even as I chided myself. At this point, I should know better. At this point, I should have been grateful he even remembered I had a game—

My body suddenly froze, foot hovering over the next stair.

I'd thought it was strange that he was more interested in high school football than he was with the fact that his only son was turning eighteen. But it wasn't until that very moment that I realized high school football was probably the precise reason my father had come home early.

Without stopping to think, I spun around on my heel and marched straight down the way I'd come. My dad was still talking on the phone, muttering in some language I didn't understand with a hand cupped over the receiver. It didn't matter. In that moment, nothing else mattered.

"They hauled a kid off the football field yesterday."

He stopped talking at once, staring up at me in surprise. The phone froze in his hand, and although the voice on the other end continued speaking he was no longer paying attention. A second later, he hung up without a word of goodbye.

"Nate Jessup," I continued in that same unaffected voice. "That was his name."

No reason not to speak in the past tense. Both he and I knew that Nate Jessup would never be setting foot in our little seaside town ever again.

My father nodded slowly, setting down the phone as he joined me at the foot of the stairs. He was a tall man, muscular and fit. I got my height and temper from him. Everything else I like to think I got from my mom. His eyes pierced me, actually seeing me for the first time.

"One of your teammates?"

Like he doesn't already know.

"One of my friends."

In hindsight, I couldn't tell you what exactly made me do it. Like most things about my dad, I knew better. But with Nate Jessup's screams forever ringing in my ears I found myself matching my father's gaze, standing in front of him toe to toe.

"So how does that work exactly?" I was on thin ice, but I didn't care. Bringing up all those things we spent my entire life determined not to say. "He's going to live out his days in a black hole somewhere? He'll never see his family again?"

Unlike me, my father had long ago mastered all emotion. There wasn't a trace anywhere on his face as he continued staring directly into my eyes.

"Yes."

I flinched. Just a single word, but it took my breath away.

In the silence that followed, I foundered while he remained strong. Shifting involuntarily from foot to foot. Trying to control my breathing, while struggling to hold his gaze. I didn't last long. After only a few agonizing seconds I broke the connection, dropping my gaze to the floor.

"That's messed up," I muttered, heading back to my room.

"What was that?"

His voice was sharp now. That impenetrable stare had given way to the anger underneath. In just a second he'd circled in front of me, blocking my retreat to the stairs.

A shiver swept over me, freezing my body perfectly still.

"I didn't mean..." Our eyes locked for a moment before I bowed my head respectfully. "I only meant, what if it was me? You and I would just never see each other—"

The fist came out of nowhere, hitting me right in the face.

A sharp cry echoed off the high ceilings as I staggered back, catching myself on the tips of my fingers before I could fall. Something warm and wet trickled down the side of my face, but before I could pull in a breath he grabbed my sleeve—yanking me roughly to my feet.

"Never talk like that again!" he commanded, glaring at me with a truly unfathomable rage. "Even as a joke, even to me. You never talk like that again—DO YOU UNDERSTAND?!"

Breathe. Take a breath, Jamie.

This was the part where I was supposed to agree. The part where I was supposed to give the obligatory 'yes, sir'. We had been down this road many times before. But for one of the first times, I couldn't seem to manage it. No matter how I tried, I couldn't seem to find the words.

My head jerked up and down.

For a split second, I was terrified this wouldn't be enough. People like my father tended to demand something more. But he released his grip on me, cocking his head towards the door before turning back to his phones.

"Take out the recycling. You forgot to roll it to the curb."

Just like that, he left me standing by the stairs. I was still bleeding, and ghostly pale. He always liked to sandwich these moments of nightmare within the mundane. How was your football game? Take out the recycling. You'd never guess what happened in between.

With robotic movements, I spun around on my heel and headed out into the cold.

Breathe, Jamie. Take a breath.

It was easier outside. With a thick door between us sheltering me. Free from those piercing eyes.

I stood on the porch for a second, pulling in silent gasps of the freezing air. Then squared my shoulders and made my way around to the side of the house.

He was right; I'd only wheeled down the trash, not the recycling. I'd been in a hurry when I'd gotten home from school. My head was still ringing as I grabbed the heavy cart and started wheeling it down the drive. Not aware of anything going on around me. Not even noticing that the beautiful girl next door was in the process of doing the same.

We froze at the same time, catching sight of each other in the dark.

Her eyes widened as they swept over my face, taking in every detail, dilating in shock when they saw the blood. For a split second, she glanced towards the house. To the shiny new car parked in the driveway, the one that hadn't been there before. When she looked back a moment later, those hazel eyes were full of silent horror. And shimmering with something akin to pity.

Neither was an emotion I was prepared to allow.

Without a single word of acknowledgement, I swept back towards the house. Swinging my hair forward to shield myself from view. Shutting the door quickly and quietly jogging up the stairs—desperate to end the wretched day once and for all.

Happy birthday to me...

A throbbing pain radiated down the side of my face, and I touched it gently with the back of my hand. It wasn't the first time this had happened, and I knew it wouldn't be the last. There was a reason I left his cars alone. There was a reason it didn't bother me when he was away.

"James."

A sudden voice rang out and I paused on the top stair.

"Yeah?"

There was a heavy pause.

"Why is there a broken lamp in the closet?"

I closed my eyes, wilting with a quiet sigh.

No, it most certainly wouldn't be the last...

I SLEPT LIGHTLY THAT night, but woke up determined to have a better day. The sun was out, it was the weekend, and my father knew how to hit in such a way so as not to leave a noticeable mark. All in all, nothing that a little caffeine and positive thinking couldn't rationalize away.

I got dressed quickly and headed downstairs. My father was already awake; I could hear a muffled voice coming from inside his study, and I deliberately quieted my steps as I slid past to the kitchen. A cup of coffee *and* a banana to ward off any lectures regarding the merits of a balanced breakfast. I was halfway out the door before I returned and dropped the banana back on the counter. I was eighteen now. I could eat and drink whatever I wanted.

A second later, I doubled back and grabbed the banana.

Only nine in the morning, but it was already coming on eighty degrees—the last hurrah of a dying season. I stretched my arms above my head, briefly considering whether I wanted to go for a run. Then, feeling the profound need to do something normal, I decided to wash my car.

Doesn't get more normal than this, I thought, backing it out into the driveway before returning to the garage for a bucket and sponge.

Since rocketing our family to the highest echelons of society, my father had developed some rather inconsistent ideas about the concepts of 'privilege' and 'class'. About some things, he was an unwavering snob. VIP lounges, season passes to sporting events we didn't attend. A private club located in Manhattan that was so exclusive the Mayor of New

York had been turned away at the door. But there were other seemingly random things he liked the idea of us doing ourselves.

Washing cars, cleaning the gutters on the roof. Whenever he was home, he waged a passive-aggressive war with the groundskeeper about who was going to mow the lawn.

With the sun beating down I sprayed the jeep from front to back and got to work with the sponge, peeling off my wet t-shirt and tossing it onto the grass.

While telling myself I didn't care, I knew the sight of me doing something like this would please him. Maybe even hold his attention long enough to remember that his only child'd had a birthday yesterday, one he was forced to spend bleeding and alone. Not that it mattered. Not that I cared.

...not that he was ever coming out of his office.

I lingered outside as long as I could, taking extra care with the tires, soaping then re-soaping the hood, casting furtive glances at the shuttered windows. When it became clear no one was noticing my little task, I finally gave up and washed it all clean. Once it was dry, I returned the supplies to the garage before snatching up my wet t-shirt and traipsing back inside.

Maybe I'll go for a run after all, I thought as I headed up to my room. *Anything to get out of the house for a while—*

"James," my father's voice echoed up the stairs, "there's someone here to see you."

I glanced instinctively over my shoulder, wondering if there was some weekend plan I'd forgotten, then jogged back down the stairs...and froze perfectly still.

Gabrielle Tanner was standing in the doorway.

What the heck?

In all my life, I'd never seen someone so pale. It was like she'd wandered next door and found herself knocking on the gates of hell. Each delicate feature was rigid with tension, and without her seeming to realize it her slender body had subconsciously angled towards the door.

I was hyperaware of my father. I was also hyperaware that I wasn't wearing a shirt.

"Hey," she greeted awkwardly.

She was holding a plate covered in a mountain of tin foil. From her manic expression, my father probably thought we were going to use the foil to make hats and contact some alien race.

For a split second, I was too surprised to move. Then I realized they were both watching me and took another step down the stairs. "Uh...hey." I resisted the urge to ask what she was doing in my house. "Dad, this is Gabrielle Tanner. I know her from...from school."

It was an abruptly awkward situation. If the man had been paying even the slightest bit of attention, he would have known she'd been our neighbor for the last fourteen years. Back when we were in elementary school, I'm sure she came by on several occasions and asked to recover her Frisbee from our yard. But like he was with most things that happened within a fifty-mile radius of his house, the man was completely oblivious.

Gabrielle seemed to realize it as well.

Her lips twitched as her eyes flashed to my face. My cheeks heated with a flush I couldn't control, but before I had a chance to feel embarrassed she was shaking his hand—introducing herself like it was for the first time.

"Gabrielle?" he asked pleasantly.

"It's Gabby." She managed a slight smile, shifting the plate so she could properly shake hands. "Nice to meet you, sir."

The contrast couldn't have been greater. The physical incarnation of every teenage nightmare, and a wide-eyed pixie who looked like she'd escaped from the set of *A Midsummer Night's Dream*. My father's eyes twinkled as he glanced between us. His moods, like his tempers, were easily changeable. They would go from dark to light at a moment's notice.

"James," he said, turning to me expectantly, a leftover smile still lingering on his face, "aren't you going to ask your friend inside?"

That's an excellent question. Am I?

I stared at Gabrielle for another second, her hands tightening on the plate.

Then, well aware that my father was still watching us, I schooled my face into a smile and gestured her upstairs with a casual tilt of my head.

She scampered away from the door with a bit too much speed, betraying the fear hidden behind that polite smile. I waited until she reached me then we climbed the rest of the stairs together, leaving my father gazing up at us from beside the door.

"Have fun, kids."

He sounded amused, as if tickled by the novelty of it. As few seconds later, I heard the telltale sound of his office door closing. Followed by the lock.

Gabrielle and I paused in the upstairs hallway and shot each other a discreet look. I still had no idea what she was doing there, and she seemed to be having a mild panic attack with the knowledge that my notorious father was prowling around somewhere in the house. My lips parted to say something reassuring, but in the end I merely cocked my head down the hall.

"My room's over there."

She nodded, and the two of us silently made our way down the hall.

In an twist of supreme mercy, the room wasn't as messy as it usually was. The second my father had come home early, I'd undergone my traditional hasty cleanup. Dirty clothes were safely hampered and left for the laundress in the basement. The bed was rumpled but made.

Still...I wasn't exactly prepared for guests.

"Do you, uh..." I stalled for time, flipping over my bloody pillow-case before scrambling around for a shirt. "Do you want something to drink?"

She stared at minute at the pillow, then shook her head.

"Actually, I brought you something."

I pulled a t-shirt over my head and looked at her. She was sitting cross-legged in the middle of the floor and gestured for me to do the same. A curious smile crooked my lips as I settled down. The plate was set between us and she removed the foil with a flourish.

For a second we sat there in silence, both staring at the plate.

Eventually, I had to ask.

"What is that?"

I hadn't realized she'd been smiling. By the time I did, it had faded from her face. A bristling scowl took its place as she shoved the plate towards my knees.

"It's a cake," she snapped. "I made it for your birthday."

My head snapped up in surprise as my mind went perfectly blank. For a few moments, I simply sat there. Then it was all I could do to parrot back the words.

"You made that for my birthday?"

It was her turn to blush. "I had some free time," she began, bristling defensively once more. "And seeing as no one else in your life cared to commemorate the occasion..."

A few years ago, that might have stung. Today I just sat there, staring down at the plate as a slow smile started spreading across my face.

"Are you sure it's a cake?"

Her eyes narrowed into a glare, but I was grinning now. In fact, I couldn't seem to stop.

"Look, if you don't want it—"

I scooped a handful out of the center and shoved it into my mouth, maintaining direct eye contact the entire time. Her mouth fell open and she stared at me in shock. Twice, her eyes flickered between my chocolatey hand and the giant crater in the cake. For a second, it looked like she was considering chiding me. Then she grabbed a handful for herself and did the same thing.

For ten minutes, we sat together on the floor.

We didn't talk. We barely looked at each other. Just snuck occasional secret glances, lips curving up at the corners. When we were finished, she picked up the plate and walked out of my room without a single word. Leaving me in a pile of questions and crumbs.

We ate the entire cake.

Chapter 9

I woke the next morning with frosting on the floor and a smile on my face. I hadn't really left the room after Gabrielle went home. I'd ducked out only to shower, but returned quickly and lingered there until sundown. Watching television, flipping absentmindedly through books, grinning with no provocation at random intervals throughout the day.

It was the first thing I thought about when the sun finally came up. The first thought that popped into my head when I opened my eyes.

I wonder what the girl next door is doing...

By the time I got dressed and ready for the day (spending far more time prepping in the mirror than usual) I had half a mind to go over there and find out.

A million half-baked excuses raced through my head as I meandered distractedly down the stairs. I thought up a million ill-conceived reasons for me to go over there and knock on her door.

I could always claim to need a bit more time on my half of the English project. But she'd never believe that since we'd wrapped the thing up just days before. I could claim I heard something suspicious, or carry up the paper before the sprinklers soaked it through. Those were all perfectly legitimate, right? Good neighborly things to do?

If only she'd left the plate. Everything would be so much easier if she'd given me the opportunity to return that freakin' plate—

"There you are!"

I jumped a mile, grabbing at the front of my shirt. This was another hazard of having my father back in the house. He'd probably aged me fifty years.

"I was just coming up to get you." He pulled me into the kitchen without really looking at my face. "Sit down—we're eating breakfast."

I froze like he'd gone mad, staring down at the steaming plates of food covering the table. There was easily enough to feed twelve people.

Everything from bagels, to croissants, to a strange combination of hash browns and eggs I was sure he'd made himself.

The only thing I didn't see was coffee. I glanced at the counter from the corner of my eye. The machine was missing from the shelf.

"Sit down, I said." He kicked out a chair. "Come on. We've done this before."

Yeah. When I was four.

"What's up?" I asked warily, reaching for the orange juice.

Our lives operated in patterns. At no point did those patterns intersect. A shared morning meal? That kind of thing wasn't supposed to happen. Even now, my father had forsaken his usual chair to sit in one a lot closer to my own.

"I got some news last night, and I just wanted to..." For one of the first times I could remember, my father couldn't finish the thought. Instead, he grabbed the plate out of my hands and began loading it up with a piece of everything on the table, dousing the entire thing in a tidal wave of maple syrup. "Here. Eat something. You're not eating enough, James."

I watched silently, keeping my hands in my lap. Finally, I swallowed. "What was the news?"

He hesitated, in the process of heaping more sausages onto my plate, and then slowly lowered the spatula back to the table. There was a moment of silence as he pulled in an inaudible breath. "The research and development branch of my company has succeeded in identifying the gene believed to cause mutations. All they require now is a sample of the subject's DNA."

A tiny frown creased my forehead as I stared in confusion. "I thought they already did that. Five years ago, when they started rounding up the mothers—"

"It was imprecise," he interrupted briskly, waving a hand. "According to the most recent studies, they have now mastered the sequencing process required to know for sure."

Imprecise? How many innocent women had fallen into the margins of that imprecision?

I nodded slowly, pushing the soggy mess of food with my fork. My father and I rarely talked these days, and when we did it certainly was never about his work. I wondered why he felt the need to share with me now. My gut twisted. Something was up. It had to be. Or could he be... excited?

"So are you guys going to start opening up closed cases?" I asked cautiously. "Re-testing some of the women with the new—"

"What's done is done." He shook his head dismissively. "We're not re-opening cases."

I stared at him for a moment, then dropped my eyes back down to my plate.

"Then...are you flying out for work?" I tried again, more confused than ever as to the reason behind the bizarre family breakfast. "For longer this time?"

He had once been gone for five straight months, rounding up a group of particularly volatile teenagers in Cuba. When he finally got back, he confessed that he'd flown in for a couple of hours somewhere in the middle. He didn't feel the need to wake me.

"No, that's...that's actually the news." Our eyes locked and he shifted uncomfortably in his chair. "Upon my company's recommendation, the federal government is adopting a policy of random testing. They've decided to start a pilot program at your school."

My lips parted and I leaned back in surprise. "At Seranto?" Of course at Seranto, it was a stupid question. I just couldn't think of anything else to say. "Why would—"

"It's one of the top five private schools, patronized by some of the most prominent and affluent families in the nation." He spoke in a monotone, reciting the party line. "The Secretary of Homeland Security is hoping to promote a 'lead by example' sort of mentality." His eyes flickered briefly to mine. "Then, of course, there was the incident last week."

Nate. This is about Nate. No. This was *about Nate.*

If a child with supernatural abilities was able to infiltrate one of the top private academies in the land, what was to stop them from going even further? One second they're playing football with your sons, the next they're having children with your daughters. Then the gene is in *your* family. Then *your* name goes on some black-ops list.

"So they're just going to start testing people?" I asked incredulously, the fork forgotten in my hand. "They'll show up at school and take samples of DNA—"

"There's still a lot to work out logistically," he interrupted, looking uncharacteristically agitated as he gestured to my plate. "Eat your breakfast, James. The food's starting to get cold."

"But I don't understand." I was crossing that line again, but at the moment I was too caught up to care. "They'll have access to the entire school? Unfettered random testing—"

"Not for at least a month," he snapped. "Now will you eat your damn—"

He raised his hand and I flinched. A silence fell over the table.

It was only after that I realized what he was trying to do. That he'd simply been reaching for the salt when I jerked back in my chair. He froze, paling as white as the curtains, then slowly retracted his hand, setting it in plain sight by his napkin.

And this is why we don't have family breakfasts.

I didn't know what to do about the silence. I didn't know what to do, period. I'd never seen my father look the way he looked right now. Staring at me with complete devastation.

"I'm allergic," I said quietly. "To the syrup."

The kitchen was suddenly cold.

I hadn't said it to guilt him, I was only trying to explain. But my father looked like I'd stabbed a knife into his chest. He stared at me a moment, then dropped his eyes to my plate. The same plate he'd loaded with food then drenched in a small ocean of maple syrup.

Twice, he started to speak. Twice, he came up blank.

"Jamie, I..."

My eyes locked on the table. At the sound of my nickname—the name my friends used—I'd gone very still. I couldn't remember the last time he'd called me Jamie. It must have been when I was a child. We sat in silence for another minute as I silently begged him to finish the sentence.

Then he pushed back from the table and walked away.

AT LEAST ONE GOOD THING had come from my disastrous family breakfast: I now had a perfectly good reason to go pester the girl next door.

"My dad hid the coffee," I said without preamble.

She blinked sleepily at me, having just opened the door. When it became clear that I was serious and this wasn't some kind of joke she opened it wider, shaking her head. "You guys have really covered the whole range of family issues, haven't you?" She gestured me inside, padding down the hall to the kitchen. "You've got little problems, you've got big problems—"

"This is a *very* big problem," I said stiffly, trying to make up for the lameness of the excuse by the sternness of my tone. "I'm already going through withdrawal."

She snorted, firing up the machine and pointing to the cabinet with the mugs. I reached up immediately and pulled two of them down, pausing slightly when I read them.

"These off-limits?"

I waved them gently to catch her attention, holding them still as she read.

World's Best Dad.

It was scrawled in messy child's penmanship, immortalized forever in paint. The mug for her mother was an even more primitive creation. Mounded together and baked in a kiln.

She froze, blushed then swept across the kitchen, taking them out of my hands and replacing them with something new. "I should really just throw those out," she murmured.

I watched each movement silently, feeling far more intrusive when it came to other people's family drama than I normally would. "They're gone a lot?"

She threw me a sharp look, then softened. Eyes fixed on the faint bruise on my cheek. "Yeah. A whole lot."

I dropped my eyes to the floor and nodded, tracing a square of tile with my shoe. "Do they check in?"

There was a hitch in her breathing but she answered with a sigh, moving swiftly around the coffee maker to fix our morning brew. "*I* call them. At least, I used to." The mugs filled up slowly, one at a time. "I've left long, rambling voicemails, if that's what you wanted to know."

My cheeks flushed as I accepted a mug. I knew the feeling all too well. It was that cold feeling of hugging someone who wasn't hugging you back. "Oh...sorry."

"Don't be," she said briskly, clinking her cup against mine. "At least I'm going to a nice school. At least I get to stay in this house."

The Tanners may have been more interesting than most, but in this respect they were exactly the same. Parents around here used money like a leash. A new car in the driveway, a vacation in France...it was the only way most of them knew how to show their love.

"The silver lining is that there are some things I'd rather they don't know about." She hopped up onto the counter, folding her legs beneath her. "Keggers, suspensions...that sort of thing."

I couldn't help but laugh, loosening up for the first time today. "You throw a lot of keggers I don't know about?"

She flashed a coy grin. "Touché. But the suspension was real."

Like most things involving Gabrielle Tanner, her eleventh-grade suspension was a bit of a legend. One day, she'd been arguing with Mrs. Montgomery about her biology grade; the next day, the lab had burned to the ground.

While the Seranto police force had been unable to find any conclusive proof, the Seranto High faculty had come to their own conclusions. Suspension was the least they could do.

"Yeah," I blurted with a smile, "I heard about that."

The second the words left my mouth I instantly regretted it. Her head snapped up with a glare, and the warm morning glow in the kitchen seemed to chill by several degrees.

"What?" she asked sharply. "That I wouldn't sleep with Eric Kaminski? So when he and his friends left a hot plate on and burned down the place, he decided to blame it on me?"

I knew Eric. This version of the story made a bit more sense.

"At any rate, you know that tech club?" she asked.

I nodded curiously. The Seranto High Institute of Technology. They'd made t-shirts last year, but they were banned for being unintentionally profane.

"They promised they could reconstruct old video feed from the science hall," she said brightly. "I'll soon be exonerated."

My face lit up with a smile as I stared down into my coffee. She had a way of making even the most dismal situations seem inexplicably light. It absolutely baffled me.

"I don't know how you do that," I said softly.

She glanced up from her mug. "Do what?"

"Stay so positive." I flushed, suddenly wishing I hadn't said anything at all. "You're always able to...to find the good."

An awkward silence fell over the kitchen as she stared at me and I stared into my mug. A full minute passed before she ventured a tentative question. "Are you okay?"

My breath caught in my chest and I lifted my head with a sigh. There were so many ways to answer. None of them were appropriate for this sunshiny day.

"My dad's company is starting a flagship program at the school," I said flatly. "Random DNA sampling. They say they're finally able to accurately isolate the gene."

She sucked in a quick breath, but otherwise stayed collected and calm. "Well, I guess that makes sense. Start a program at one of the most prestigious schools in the country. Attended by the commandant's own son." Our eyes met briefly before she glanced down at the coffee, swishing it casually in her cup. "Is it because of Nate? They think there are more people like him enrolled at our school?"

I shifted restlessly, suddenly wishing I hadn't brought it up. "Yeah, I think so."

She nodded again, her lips thinning into a hard line. "I guess that makes sense, too. It always starts with one..."

I LEFT GABRIELLE'S house shortly after and wandered around a while on my own. I was unwilling to stay and continue the conversation. Unwilling to return to my house, where my father was no doubt hard at work making the world a 'safer' place.

I walked past the local grocery store, already decked out in navy and white streamers, preparing for the next football game. The names of the team had been scribbled beneath their jersey numbers on the wall. Someone had circled mine with a magic marker heart.

A few minutes later, I wandered past Nate Jessup's house. The driveway was full of moving boxes and there was a sign on the lawn. I pulled down my hood and hurried past before his father or two brothers could come outside.

Eventually my aimless meandering took me all the way down to the beach, where I waited out the bulk of the day in isolation, staring out at the waves.

Considering how many things were spinning around in my head, my mind couldn't settle on any one particular thought. It was all just feelings. Hazy indistinct feelings, so dissonant and repressed that trying to isolate one was like trying to remember a dream. I let them wash over me, whatever they were, wrapping my arms around my chest with my feet in the sand.

Time passed slowly.

I sat on a bluff above the rest of the shoreline, watching dogs jump in and out of the frothy surf, watching screaming children bury each other's toys in the sand.

Strange as it sounds, it took me almost a full afternoon to realize I was sad. Desperately sad, with the kind of heartache I hadn't felt in a long time. It stung the corners of my eyes as I gazed out at the sparkling water, whispering things in my ear I couldn't yet understand.

By the time I got home, the sky was beginning to darken. My skin was chilled to the bone with the evening wind, and my time at the beach had left me feeling strangely subdued.

I walked slowly up the driveway, hands in my pockets, and looked up with surprise as the front door burst open and my father hurried out. There was a briefcase in one hand and a phone in the other. Our eyes met and his skin blanched the color of yellowed chalk.

"I'm going out," he said unnecessarily. Was that an apology in his voice? I couldn't be sure. "There's Chinese take-out in the fridge. Make sure you eat something."

I nodded, trying to think of something meaningful to say. Anything better than what I ended up going with. "Drive safe."

Really?

He slipped past me with a curt nod of his head and climbed into the Benz, revving the engine and streaking away in the dark before I could even lift a hand in goodbye.

I stood in the driveway, staring down the street a long time after he left.

Chinese take-out. That's what I should be doing. Having some dinner and going to bed. Trying not to dream.

Less than a minute later I was standing on Gabrielle Tanner's porch, knocking with quiet urgency. There were soft footsteps then she opened the door, staring at me in surprise.

"What did you mean, it always starts with one...?"

Chapter 10

For the second time in twenty-four hours, Gabrielle and I sat cross-legged in the middle of my bedroom floor. This time, there was no cake between us. This time, there were no smiles.

"I've been tracking it in towns all over the country," Gabrielle said quietly, fingers flying over the keys on my laptop. "Every time it's exactly the same. Some kid will be found in exactly the right place, at exactly the right time."

My eyes glowed with the light of the screen, trying to follow along as dozens of news articles popped up one after the other. "Exactly the right time for who?"

She glanced at me, and then turned the screen my way. "For your father's company."

Recovery of Diplomat's Son Opens Doors at U.N.
Arrest Shakes German Parliament to the Core

One right after another scrolled past on the screen. Every headline was exactly the same.

Each time Obtero, my father's company, hit a roadblock in terms of expansion, each time some country or organization stood in their way—people with abilities would be discovered at the heart of such opposition, and it would magically fall away. Leaving nothing in their path.

It could be a judge's daughter in Denver or a senator's son in Rome.

"There are over three hundred articles here," I murmured, scrolling through the list. My eyes flitted to her face. "How long have you been working on this?"

"Here. Look at this." She pushed back her hair, guiding my hand to a specific op-ed near the bottom of the list. "You see? This started all the way back in the nineties. That's the first time a person was identified as having 'abilities beyond the capacity of a regular human'. There was a huge push to establish a commission to track people with similar powers, but the case was shot down by a Supreme Court Justice in '92. Four weeks later, his niece was discovered to have the gene."

I read over her shoulder with a frown.

"Due to an undisclosed personal bias, Judge Remmers is hereby removed from the case and his decision deemed null and void. Pending further investigation, the commission tasked with tracking said enhanced individuals will proceed according to schedule. Whether or not Remmers will face prosecution is in the hands of the court..."

My voice trailed off as I glanced at the side of her head. "Gabby...how long have you been working on this?"

"One in five hundred people have the gene, Jamie." She swiveled around to face me, the light from the monitor shining in her eyes. "That's about fourteen million people all around the world. It isn't a stretch that some of them would belong to some pretty influential families—but this? This goes a little deeper than that."

"*Gabby.*" I slammed the computer shut, facing her straight on. "How long?"

Her mouth opened, but the words wouldn't come. A strange tension strained the edges of her eyes, and without seeming to think about it she glanced back towards her house.

I softened, and then sighed.

"This is your parents' research. Not yours."

She bit her lip, looking ready to deny it. Then slowly nodded.

"I thought they were travel writers, or something."

"They were travel consultants; they wrote about places they went to and stuff," she answered softly. "Now they're something else."

The two of us lapsed into tense silence. Both wondering how much we could actually trust the other. Both wondering how much we could actually say.

The irony wasn't lost on either of us. The commandant's son poring over twenty years of damning evidence with the daughter of the couple writing the exposé.

There was only one problem. I didn't see it that way.

"I get what you're saying," I began slowly. "I get that it's strange, but..."

She leaned forward, waiting for the rest. "But?"

"But they all *had* abilities," I concluded apologetically. "That part wasn't faked."

She shook her head, convinced she wasn't hearing correctly. "So—"

"—so what does it matter?"

The words rang out between us as we each took a mental step back. I stared at her, she stared at me, and in the silence that followed I instinctively knew that something had changed.

Then, with what looked like great determination, she squared her shoulders and replied, "What's the mantra of your father's company?" she asked quietly. "The very foundation upon which Obtero was built?"

I remained silent while she chanted the words aloud. Reciting them verbatim, the way we'd all been taught to do in school.

"Equality." Her lips turned up at the irony, thinning with a hard smile that didn't reach her eyes. "We shall find them in the cities, we shall find them in the schools, we shall find them in their homes. Together, we shall find them. And cleanse our world anew."

I'd probably heard those words a thousand times before, but they'd never really struck me until that very moment. There was tension in my voice when I replied. A tone that was definitely not there before.

"What exactly are you saying?"

"You want to support what your father's doing? Fine." Her eyes glowed as she jabbed her finger at the computer. "But this isn't unbiased or equal. This isn't the 'random selection' they'd have us believe. This is an *agenda*. And now..."

She trailed off, letting me finish the sentence for myself.

"...they've come here."

A shiver ran up my spine, and I found myself suddenly relieved that my father wasn't in the house. In fact, I found myself worried about when exactly he might be coming home.

"But why?" I asked quietly, unable to keep that worry from my voice. "If they're targeting people to deflect and destabilize, to progress the agenda of the corporation, why come here?"

Gabrielle's eyes shone with unspeakable pity as they locked onto my face. "Jamie..."

"This is the last place in the world they should be looking," I continued, fighting a rising feeling of panic. "You'd never find a city more supportive of the cause."

"That's right," she said slowly, making a careful study of my eyes. "There's a lot in this town that's important to them. A lot of people who have a lot to lose."

"We have to find out," I said, suddenly pushing to my feet. Her head snapped up in surprise as I grabbed her wrists, pulling her up with me. "Whatever it is they're looking for, we have to find out what it is."

"...*who* it is," she corrected quietly.

I could barely hear her over the ringing in my ears. My world had narrowed with tunnel-vision focus, and I suddenly knew exactly what I had to do.

"Come on." I took her by the hand. "I know where to start looking..."

REMEMBER HOW I'M A teenage boy who has *never once* touched the Lamborghini sitting in his own garage? Remember how I had a virtual panic attack eating pizza outside of the kitchen?

So imagine how much I wanted to break into my father's office.

"Can you check again?" I asked quietly, staring at the room at the end of the hall.

Gabrielle looked over at me, and then glanced back towards the front door. "Seriously? I've already checked like five times—"

"Please?"

She stifled a sigh then doubled back the way we'd come, kneeling on the couch so that she could stare through a crack in the curtains. "It's all clear. There's no one on the street."

That should have comforted me.

It didn't.

"This is a bad idea," I murmured, unable to take my eyes off the door.

We'd been standing there a full five minutes, but short of sending Gabrielle repeatedly to check for my father I'd yet to make any progress towards the office door. Every time I tried, it was like something short-circuited in my brain. My feet simply refused to move forward.

"This was *your* idea," she prompted quietly.

"Yeah, but maybe we shouldn't do it."

She bit her lip, trying to rein in her frustration. "Why don't I just do it myself? You can stand watch by the window, and tell me if he comes back—"

"*No*," I interrupted quickly.

I could only imagine what my father would do if he caught *me* breaking into his office. I didn't want to imagine what he'd do to a stranger instead.

"I'll-I'll do it. We'll do it together," I amended quickly. "It's just..." My voice trailed off as the hallway seemed to elongate before my very eyes. "...maybe you should check again."

I didn't know why she was smiling, and I startled when she slipped her hand into mine.

"There's no one here, Jamie. Just us." She gave my hand a little squeeze. "Let's go."

Without another word, she released me and started walking silently down the hall. My heart clenched at the sight of it, but I couldn't let her go alone. With a million profanities ringing in my head, I jogged to catch up with her and we continued on together.

The second I was close enough, she laced her fingers back through mine.

"Is it going to be locked?" she asked softly as we reached the door.

"No," I assured, reaching for the handle, "he knows I would nev-er—"

My voice cut off and my hand froze.

Of all the idiotic, masochistic, spur-of-the-moment shenanigans I'd concocted over the course of my life, this had to be the very worst. My heart was pounding so fast it was making me light-headed, and the side of my face was throbbing where my father's fist had struck me just a day before. A visible tremor swept through my body, and Gabrielle shot me a sideways look.

"I could always check the street again," she offered with a coaxing smile. "You've made me do it twenty-three times already. Why not make it twenty-four?"

Twenty-four. Same as Nate's jersey number.

My spine stiffened as I stared down at her with a peculiar expression. I wasn't sure whether she'd done it on purpose. Probably not—the girl couldn't have been less interested in sports. But the second she said the words, another voice rang through my mind. It was the voice of a faceless man behind a helmet. Pointing a gun at one of my childhood friends.

'He's here on the football field. Number twenty-four. All clear for ex-traction.'

The gun cracked and I winced with the ghost of the impact, re-membering exactly how it felt when Nate Jessup crumpled to the ground.

And just like that, my mind was made up. Just like that, I squared my shoulders, pulled in a faltering breath, and opened the door...

I HALF-EXPECTED AN alarm to go off the second I stepped inside. For a SWAT team to descend from the ceiling with their weapons drawn, or a million red dots to appear on my chest.

But nothing happened.

The office looked exactly the way I'd always imagined it. Dark leather chairs, an imposing desk, and floor-to-ceiling shelves full of books I'd never read. It was tasteful, yet sparse. A little cold and impersonal. Much like the man who spent all his time there.

Gabrielle and I stopped in the middle of the floor and looked around.

"Where does he keep his files?" she asked quietly.

"I don't know," I realized, wrapping my arms around my chest, "I've never been in here before."

Her eyes widened in surprise as she momentarily suspended the search.

"Like, *ever*?"

The arms came down and I shot her a look. "Why would I have ever been in here?"

There was a pause.

"That's a good point."

A sudden wave of anxiety swept over me and I gestured about with an impatient hand.

"Can we just hurry, please? He could seriously be back any second."

She turned away from me, resisting the urge to roll her eyes. "Why do I feel like you've already said that? Like a thousand times..."

Together, the two of us roamed in a slow circle around the room. Pausing to examine anything that might be of importance. Taking special care not to disturb anything on the desk.

For the most part, there wasn't much. Just a few scattered pieces of correspondence, nothing of particular interest that he wouldn't tell me if I'd asked. The computer was highly tempting, but not only were we missing the password but I was terrified it would somehow record our keystrokes even if we were able to miraculously log on.

"Gabby," I whispered, instinctively lowering my voice, "I'm not sure what—"

A sudden sound made me stop cold: the sound of tires speeding down the road.

The two of us froze, and then dropped to the floor. Covering our heads as a pair of headlights flashed in through the window. Covering our mouths as we fought the urge to scream. For a second, nothing happened. Then a pair of voices drifted in from outside.

"—told you we were heading the wrong way! Jen told us to turn on Tressaway Street, not Tressmen. You should have used the friggin' navigator!"

"I was the one who said Tressaway all along! You told me not—"

"Just turn the car around! We're going to be late!"

There was a screech of rubber tires, then the headlights vanished. Leaving the two of us lying like statues on the floor. We stayed there for a long time. Probably a lot longer than was normal. Then slowly, very slowly, we managed to pull in a breath.

...holy hot tamales.

Gabrielle started giggling, but my skin had gone ice cold.

"We need to get out of here," I said with sudden urgency. "We need to leave."

She stopped laughing long enough to register the look on my face. "Jamie, relax. It was just some random car, nobody's—"

"*Now*," I insisted. "We need to leave *now*."

I grabbed hold of her wrist and started pulling her towards the door, but she yanked herself free, holding up a soothing hand. "Listen, I understand how—"

"No, you *don't* understand," I said sharply, a lot more sharply than I'd intended. "You don't understand what he'll do."

A sudden silence descended on the room, thinning the air and making it hard to breathe. I felt her eyes on me, but kept mine on the floor. I was too ashamed to speak, too stricken to move.

"Jamie," she finally murmured, taking a step closer, "how long has your dad hit you?"

My eyes shot up as a wave of molten defiance burned through my veins. For a second, I actually forgot my fear of being discovered as I glared down at her with all my might. "I don't know what you're talking about."

She flinched, looking frightened but unbearably sympathetic at the same time. "I'm sorry, I wasn't trying to—"

I pulled back as she reached for me again, wondering how I'd let her talk me into something like this. "It doesn't matter. We just need to go."

"Jamie, I—"

"Seriously, Tanner, I don't care. Let's just get out of—"

"No, *look*." She pointed behind me to the shelves. "I think I found something."

I followed her gaze to a tiny piece of paper tucked between one of the books. It wasn't so much a message as a series of random words, scrawled across the page.

831966712

Sackville Bank, Grand Cayman

$4,000,000

We stared at the paper for a moment, reading it over several times, then she lifted her gaze to my face. "What is this?"

I shook my head, staring numbly at the writing. "I have no idea."

That's when we heard the front door open. And my heart stopped beating.

IN A SINGLE MOMENT, I felt all the blood rush from my face—leaving me so light-headed, I thought I might black out. The walls tilted precariously as I reached out and grabbed Gabrielle by the sleeve, pulling her away from the door.

"James?" a quiet voice drifted down the hallway.

Oh, crap!

My hand came up over my mouth as the logic centers of my brain splintered into a million pieces. Gabrielle was standing beside me, too frightened to move. In hellish slow motion, the progression of his movements played out like a nightmare before my eyes.

He would empty his pockets; take off his shoes by the door. The coat would go on the rack and the briefcase would go in his office. That was always the first stop he made. His office.

Leave! We need to leave!

Without saying a word I grabbed Gabrielle's hand, pointing towards the door. She nodded quickly and followed in my shadow, but a second before we slipped outside she grabbed the note we'd found and stuffed it into her pocket.

I froze in the doorway, too conflicted to move.

"What are you doing?!" I whispered furiously. "Put it back!"

She shook her head quickly, though she was trembling where she stood. There was movement in the entryway, the faint jingle of keys. My head turned automatically towards the sound before whipping back to the traitor beside me. In an act of desperation I actually tried snatching it out of her jacket, but she twisted away, knocking into the door in the process.

There was a soft *thud*, and my father called out again.

"James?"

He was walking towards us now, cutting off our only means of escape.

My body froze as my heart started pounding in my chest. There was nothing else on this side of the house. No possible reason for us to be here. The windows in the office were welded shut, and even if we could force them open we'd never make it in time.

There were only a few seconds left. Already, he was rounding the corner to the hall. The two of us locked eyes, and for a suspended moment time itself seemed to stop.

Then I did the only thing I could think of.

I kissed her.

Chapter 11

There were no words, there was just *feeling*. A million contrasting feelings coursed through my body. And each one was more overpowering than the next.

The soft curl of her hair between my fingers was like touching the finest silk. The taste of her lips on mine was like heaven itself. A cold sweat broke over my forehead at the sound of my father's voice, but my skin, wherever she touched it, was hot and flushed. Our bodies crushed together in a controlled sort of panic. Clinging as much as clutching. Panting with both fear and desire. My eyes snapped shut when her teeth brushed into my lip, and the next thing I knew we were falling back against the office door with the same dull *thud* my father must have heard when he first came inside.

Her hands slid up against my shirt. My lips were against hers. For a second, it seemed possible to pretend that my father wasn't there. That it was just her and me. That she wanted this.

Then a throat cleared quietly from the other end of the hall.

"James."

We sprang apart like we'd been burned. Panting softly. Hastily straightening clothes, smoothing down hair, and appearing very much like two horny teenagers—caught in an act of basic adolescence. *Not* searching for government secrets behind my father's back.

"Dad!" I was completely unable to catch my breath. My only hope was that it would help bolster my story. "What are you...I mean..." My cheeks flushed bright red as I dropped my eyes to the floor. "I didn't hear you come home."

"Clearly." He took a step forward, his eyes twinkling but sharp.

I had seen that look many times. It was the look he got when he was trying to make up his mind about me.

It usually didn't end well.

"Aren't you going to..."

"Oh—right." I gestured bashfully to the girl beside me, wishing very much we could both simply disappear. "Uh...you remember Gabby?"

The eyes were definitely twinkling now. In fact, it looked as though he was enjoying himself a great deal. "Of course. It's nice to see you again, Miss Tanner."

She was brave, I had to give her that. You'd never know from her voice that she had a top-secret note stashed in her back pocket. You could barely tell she was trembling.

"Hi, Mr. Hunt." She dropped my hand with a guilty flush, reaching around to pull down the back of her shirt. "Sorry to be over so late."

"Not at all," he said pleasantly. "It looks like you and my son found a way to pass the time..."

Definitely enjoying himself.

My eyes snapped shut as Gabrielle flushed again.

"Yeah, I-I should probably be getting home." She nervously tucked her hair behind her ears, skittering around him with a tight smile. "See you later, Jamie."

I lifted an awkward hand, still frozen where I stood. "'Bye."

Our eyes locked for the briefest of moments, then she was gone. Leaving me alone in the middle of my worst nightmare. Sporadically trembling and barely able to breathe.

My father stared at me. I stared at the floor by his feet.

What am I supposed to do? What am I supposed to say?

While the two of us had technically lived together for the last eighteen years, we had remarkably little experience when it came to these kinds of father-son moments. I found myself without a script, wracking my brain for anything that could get me through it unscathed.

In the end, I shocked us both. I went on the offensive.

"Why did you have to say that?" I demanded.

His eyebrows lifted and he actually took a step back in surprise. "Excuse me?"

"That we...*found a way to pass the time.*" I scowled, and fussed unnecessarily with my clothes. "Like this wasn't traumatizing enough..."

There was a split second of silence—a second where I thought my heart might literally explode—then he threw back his head with a sudden burst of laughter.

"Oh, Jamie..."

I froze with rapt attention, silently taking in every detail. As strange as it sounded, I couldn't remember the last time I'd seen my father laugh. I was sure it had to have happened at some point, we'd been together for so many years, but I truly couldn't remember.

He looked different when he laughed. Like someone I recognized only from faded photographs. The ones that had been long since locked away.

"You think this was traumatic for *you?*" He was still chuckling, shaking his head. "You didn't just see your son feeling up some girl in the hallway."

"I wasn't—" I started to deny it, then shook my head with a sullen glare. Best to play the petulant teenager card, if we were lapsing into stereotypes. "It wasn't like that."

"Then what was it like?" He snapped on the light switch with a grin, taking in every mortifying detail while casually blocking my escape down the hall. "She fell...you caught her?"

"No," I protested, "it was just—"

Wait a second...

I trailed off, staring at him in a whole new light.

...is he teasing me?

The thought had never crossed my mind. If laughing was rare, then light-hearted banter was nonexistent. But it seemed we were breaking every rule tonight. And not a moment too soon.

"Go ahead. Laugh it up." A tiny grin crept up the side of my face as I found myself both relieved and oddly heartbroken at the same time. "I live to entertain."

How was he laughing *now*? How was he teasing *now*?

"Bless you for that." He took another moment to collect himself, looking me up and down with a smile I'd swear was borderline affectionate. "So this girl..."

The grin vanished from my face and I found myself subconsciously looking towards the exits. All jokes aside, the *last* thing I wanted to do right now was talk about Gabby.

"She's nobody," I said dismissively, praying for some kind of diversion. Where the hell were those phones when I needed them? "Just a girl from school."

"Didn't look like nobody." He folded his arms across his chest, pursing his lips with that same inexplicable smile. "She's pretty. Is she your girlfriend?"

Seriously—ANY kind of diversion would be welcome right now.
Flash flood. Meteor. Pack of wild dogs.

"No, she's just..." I trailed off, raking back my hair while carefully avoiding those twinkling eyes. "I don't know. It's complicated."

He nodded knowingly, thoroughly amused by the whole situation. "Ah, one of those."

I thought that might be the end of it. I thought there was a chance I might actually get to walk away. Then, without a word of warning, he hit me with the million-dollar question.

"How did the two of you end up down here?"

By my office.

He'd been saving this question. I could tell. My father was a master interrogator; I'd seen him work many times.

Fortunately, it wasn't that hard to stretch the truth.

What was I doing in this hallway? What was I doing breaking into his office? Searching for secret documents? Risking everything for a girl I hardly even knew?

My eyes flew around the forbidden corridor before coming up blank. "I...I honestly don't know."

Maybe it was the fact that I was telling the truth. Maybe it was the wild eyes and bruised lips. Maybe it was simply the fact that there was *no way* I would dare lie to him otherwise.

But my father believed me. "Got a little carried away?"

I let out a breath, unable to control my relief. "...something like that."

With another chuckle he took a step back, gesturing me to freedom. I hesitated for a split second, unable to believe it was true, then made a bee-line for the stairs. Trying my best to keep a measured speed. Failing spectacularly. I had almost made it, when his hand shot out and grabbed my arm. My breath caught in my throat, every muscle braced for impact.

"James...you know if you get that girl pregnant, this becomes less of a conversation and more of a ritual sacrifice, right?"

I couldn't believe it. Teasing—even now.

Well, sort of teasing.

"Yes, sir."

I nodded hastily and kept my eyes on the floor. By my calculations, I had about forty seconds before I passed out from belated shock. I had to get upstairs before that happened.

Let go. Please let go.

"All right. Get out of here." He released me with a grin. At this point, I wouldn't have been surprised if he ruffled my hair. "Go be seventeen somewhere else."

I flashed him a quick look then darted to the stairs, taking them four at a time as I raced up to my room. He'd totally missed my birthday. I was eighteen now, but I wasn't about to remind him of that. Not now. This time, I made it all the way to the landing before he called out again. "I should have known...about the syrup."

I froze perfectly still, eyes burning a hole into the wall. After a moment, I glanced over my shoulder. He was standing exactly where I'd left him, speaking quietly to the floor.

"Your mother wouldn't even keep it in the house."

My teeth sank into my bottom lip. *Hard.* A second later, I tasted blood.

On the list of things my mother would have come to hate about my father, maple syrup didn't even make the top fifty. But he was trying. And bad things happened when he stopped.

"It's cool." Our eyes met and I forced a smile. "Thanks for making breakfast." Then I went out on a limb. "Now if we could only find the missing coffee maker..."

He let out a bark of laughter, surprising us both. For a fleeting moment his face warmed, and it was easy to see what I'd been missing. The man I should have been looking at all these years. It faded into a melancholy smile as he tipped his head.

"Goodnight, James."

"'Night."

I vanished before anything could ruin it. Before the other shoe could drop.

Before those tears prickling at the corners of my eyes had a chance to fall...

PANIC CAUGHT UP WITH me inside the safety of my room. I slumped back against the door. Hands cupped over my mouth. Skin, clammy and pale. Hyperventilating quietly.

It took me a few seconds to recover my balance. Then, on instinct, I found myself moving to the window—peering through the shadowy trees. There was only one light on in the house next door. Just a soft diffused glow of lamplight in the bedroom directly across from mine.

At that point, I shouldn't have been surprised to see the window open.

To reveal Gabrielle staring back at me with a question reflected in her eyes.

Are you okay?!

She didn't have to ask the question out loud. Her eyes were practically screaming it at me. Even from such a distance that hazel glowed in the moonlight, shining with silent fear.

I wished I could reassure her. I wished I could say something to make it better. But the second our eyes met in the darkness, I had a better idea. One that instantly took hold in my brain.

I am going to strangle her with my bare hands.

I jumped straight out my open window. She vanished from hers with a little shriek.

In hindsight, it probably wasn't the best idea to go sneaking out of my house right after narrowly escaping the wrath of my father. But my brain was no longer working properly. It had stopped right around the time the front door opened and I heard him call my name.

It had turned off entirely when I pulled her in for that kiss—but that was irrelevant. The girl was going to be dead soon. No point dwelling on the past.

"*Gabrielle.*" My voice hissed through the darkness. I was already standing on her front porch. Didn't risk knocking, but I knew she could hear. "Open the door."

There was a series of muffled noises from inside, along with a whispered, "*Shit!*" It would have been funny if it wasn't so serious. As it stood, I was in no mood to play games. Both hands grabbed the handle as I pressed my forehead against the wood.

"I'm not kidding, open the door." My eyes flickered through the grove of trees to my own house, where my father was no doubt locked away in his office. Perhaps he was already looking for the missing piece of paper. The one she stole. "Open it—or I kick it down."

There was a pause on the other side of the door before I heard her say:

"Can you actually do that?"

Both fists pounded into the wood with renewed rage.

"For frick's sake, Gabby! Open the da—"

The sound of breaking glass followed by a soft gasp froze me in my tracks. My breath caught in my chest and I leaned closer, pressing my ear against the door.

"...Gabby?"

More breaking glass. This time with a whimper of pain.

CRASH!

Turns out I could kick down the door after all.

"Hey!"

My eyes found her immediately, crouched at the foot of the stairs, kneeling beside what looked like an overturned armoire with her bloody arm clutched against her chest. Her eyes widened in shock as I raced forward before fixing on the door with astonishment.

"Are you...are you *crazy*?"

I ignored her, searching for the source of the blood.

"What happened? Are you okay?"

She shoved my hands aside, shakily pushing to her feet. "That was the *door* to my *house*!" She nudged the splintered planks incredulously with her toe. "I *need* one of those!"

"Gabby, what happened to your—"

"Unbelievable," she gasped, unable to look away. "I can't believe you just—"

I caught her roughly by the shoulders, spinning her back around. *"Are you okay?"*

Each word was stern. Forceful. The way my father used to speak to me on the random occasion I would get hurt as a child. There was blood smeared over the front of her sweater. That armoire hadn't just fallen over by itself.

She stared at me for another moment, then jerked her head up and down. "Yeah, I just...I just cut my hand. No big deal."

That was an awful lot of blood for *no big deal.*

"Let me see," I demanded.

There was a pause.

"Let you *see*?!" she repeated in disbelief. "How about we talk about my *freaking door*! I can't believe you did that, Jamie! What if a raccoon gets in here?!"

Another pause.

"Out of everything that could possibly get into your house you're scared of...a raccoon?"

"I don't know!" She threw up her hands, showering the carpet between us with drops of fresh blood. "Why do people *have* doors?! To keep out rodents and prowlers and such!"

While making a concentrated effort not to laugh I caught her gently by the wrist, bending down to examine the wide gash running up the side of her hand.

"This doesn't look too deep," I murmured. "You probably won't need any stitches." My eyes flickered to the overturned armoire. "What were you doing anyway?"

"I was dragging it over to make a barricade!" she snapped, yanking her arm back to her side. "In case some lunatic got the idea to start *breaking off parts of my house*!"

A guilty silence fell between us as my eyes dropped to the floor. In hindsight, it did seem a little extreme. "Okay," I began reasonably, "so in my very limited defense I was just—"

"What happened to your mouth?" she interrupted, lifting my chin to get a better look at my face. Her eyes widened when they saw my bloody lip. "Did *I*..."

Her voice choked off and both of us looked away at the same time. She had bitten me pretty hard. Right around the time I was sliding my hand up her shirt.

"No," I finally answered, staring determinedly at the floor. "That wasn't you."

At first she looked relieved. Then her lovely face paled white as snow.

"Then was it...?" She trailed off, too afraid to finish the sentence. "Did he—"

"No, he didn't," I interrupted, unwilling to even discuss the possibility. It did, however, remind me of why I'd come over in the first place. "No thanks to you."

She took a giant step back as I fixed her with a withering glare.

"What the hell were you *thinking*, taking that paper from the shelf?"

Her face paled some more, but she stood firm. "I was thinking that we went down there looking for things that didn't add up, and we found something. It's not like I was just going to leave it behind—"

"It wasn't up to you!" I interrupted. "It wasn't your decision!"

"Jamie," she began quietly, "you have to realize what that paper—"

"Give it back," I demanded, either unwilling or unable to let her finish. "Give it back to me right now. It's bad enough I'm going to have to sneak in there *again* just to return it."

"*Jamie*," she tried again, speaking with a mix of patience and caution that I didn't fully understand. "Why do you think—"

"I don't care, all right?" I was shouting now, unable to stop. "This whole stupid crusade of your parents'—I don't care! It has *nothing* to do with me—"

"It has *EVERYTHING* to do with you!" she cried, curling her fingers into fists. "How is it *POSSIBLE* that you still don't—"

She broke off with a sudden cry, hopping around in a little circle. A second later, she smacked me for good measure. Then cried out again.

I froze dead still, staring like she might have lost her mind. Then a spattering of blood rained down between us and I understood.

"Come on," I said softly. "We should bandage that."

When I reached for her, she didn't pull away. She simply stood there and let me take her arm, watching as I wrapped my sweater around it to temporarily stop the blood. She didn't say a word as I led her to the bathroom. Stayed quiet as I rinsed it off in the sink. She hardly even looked at me until our fingers touched and an electric blue spark leapt from my hand.

What the heck?

I stared down in amazement, unable to reconcile what I'd just seen. It was more than just static. It was something far, far bigger than that. But, stranger still, it didn't even hurt.

Without thinking about it I released her hand and raised my own, turning it slowly in front of my face. It looked normal. Nothing different on the outside, and yet...

"Jamie?"

I lifted my head to see her staring right at me, a look of breathless anticipation on her face. Whatever she saw on mine must have been a sight to see, because she immediately swallowed her next sentence. Instead, she slipped off the sink and took me by the hand.

"Come on, I want to show you something..."

WE WENT UP TO THE ROOF.

I didn't know why. I didn't know why I had followed her. Why I hadn't just run straight back outside—there wasn't even a door to stop me. I could have been back in my room by now.

Safely ensconced behind a locked door. Hands buried securely beneath my pillow.

But here I was. No matter how hard I tried to stay away, I kept finding myself with Gabrielle Tanner. Usually scared out of my mind. Often standing on the roof.

"My parents aren't travel writers," she blurted without warning.

"Wait, what?" My hands were tingling. I was having trouble catching my breath.

"I mean, they were...but they left. *Permanently.*" She stressed the word slightly, willing me to understand. "They've been gone for a long time."

I stared at her, shivering slightly in the cold.

"Well, that's..." It took me a second to switch gears; she was always saying the very last thing I expected. "I'm sorry, Gabby. That's terrible. When did they leave?"

She gave me a long look. "Five years ago."

My head was buzzing. Something didn't feel right. I was vaguely aware that she was still talking. I was even more vaguely aware that it was important, and highly personal. I nodded, only half following whatever she had said.

"I'm sorry," I said again. "Have you told anyone—"

"Jamie." She squared her shoulders, pulled in a deep breath, and looked me right in the eyes. "They left *five* years ago. The first day of the purge."

There was a beat of silence.

"Wait, *what*?"

Then she was falling.

I didn't know how it happened. The whole thing happened too fast for me to see. One second she was standing beside me. The next, her foot caught on a loose tile and she was tumbling over the side of the roof—hair flying up around her, arms stretched out to the sides.

I remembered thinking she looked like an angel. She was peaceful, even when she was falling straight to her death. I remembered thinking I'd miss her. That I'd really like to kiss her one more time.

And then...I was catching her.

Like something out of a dream, my mother's voice drifted through my mind.

'And the little boy realized that his world was upside-down. That he'd only dreamt he'd fallen asleep. That he'd lived in the woods the whole time.'

"I knew it," Gabrielle whispered. Her arms were wrapped around my neck and she was beaming like she'd never really seen me before. "I knew you were one of us."

I had never been more terrified in my entire life.

Chapter 12

"Jamie! Wait!"

I took off down the street without any clear destination, sprinting along the dotted yellow line. My head felt so light, it was a miracle I was still conscious. My legs were shaking so hard, it was a miracle they were keeping me upright. I couldn't breathe. I couldn't think. I couldn't focus.

"Jamie! Come back!"

A Mercedes flew around the corner and almost hit me. The horn echoed in the night long after it had passed. I kept running. The wind was rustling in my hair, the orange glow of the streetlights reflected in my terror-stricken eyes.

"Slow down! Please!"

I didn't know where I was going, but my feet seemed to have a better idea. They took me straight to the park at the end of the block, stopping abruptly right where that old fountain used to be. The one I was now positive my father had torn down.

I stared without blinking at the grass. Convinced I could still see the outline. The memory of that day suddenly coming back to haunt me, grabbing at my chest, choking me.

"Jamie!" Gabrielle skidded to a stop behind me. Clearly, she was afraid to let me out of her sight. But she was afraid to get too close. It took me a second to realize what she was holding. The jacket I'd left on the roof.

On the roof.

All at once, the memory attacked me. Stealing my breath. Shredding my voice. "What the—!"

The mind will do amazing things to protect itself. Rationalize, compartmentalize, deny, and revise. But this? I recalled each second to nightmarish perfection.

Then I threw up.

"...oh, sweetie."

Cool hands swept my hair off my forehead, rubbing gentle circles on my back as I fought to pull in a breath. The world swayed dizzily around me.

I stared in terror at my own hands. "This can't be real..."

I wasn't sure if I'd said the words aloud or in my head.

Gabrielle seemed to guess them either way. Her eyes tightened as she draped the coat over my shaking arms. "I know it seems overwhelming," she said softly. "I know it seems like the world just came crashing down. But *trust* me, things will get better."

I couldn't hear her. I couldn't hear anything over the sudden ringing in my ears.

"...I don't know what just happened."

Her eyes tightened again but she pulled in a shaky breath, forcing herself to be calm. "Yes, you do."

We locked eyes for a split second before I doubled over at the waist, hands on my knees. "Oh shit...No. No, no no..."

She knelt beside me. "Breathe, Jamie. Just breathe."

I jerked away from her hand. "Don't touch me."

She straightened up slowly, tears shining in her eyes. "Okay...I won't touch you. I'm just going to stand here, all right? I'm right here."

The world blinked in and out of focus. I was breathing too quickly. Pulling in too much air. In the back of my head I heard my father's voice, screaming at me as a child.

'You climbed up there, right? Remember you CLIMBED up there.'

A dry sob ripped through me and I crouched where I stood.

"No, this can't...this can't be happening." My hands slid over my face, tangling weakly in my hair. "There has to be something...I can't do this."

I can't BE this. I know what will happen.

"It's okay," Gabrielle soothed quietly, tears spilling down her face. "I promise—"

"You knew." My hands came down suddenly and I stared at her, eyes burning with betrayal as I connected it for the first time. "You already knew."

She pulled in a deep breath, then nodded. "Yes."

I flinched. Hearing someone else acknowledge it made it a thousand times worse.

"Why didn't...why didn't you tell me?!"

My voice echoed angrily off the quiet houses, and she cast a nervous look around before lowering her voice. "How could I say anything, with your dad living right next door?"

...my dad.

A thrill of terror shot through me as I looked back towards my house. Sitting there so innocently. Lights on in the windows.

"You-you can't tell." All of a sudden, I was a blur of movement. Clutching her hands as I stared desperately into those hazel eyes. "Gabby—*please*. You can't say anything."

She stared up at me in horror, frantically shaking her head. "Of course not! Jamie, I would never tell anyone!"

I only held on tighter, trembling from head to toe. The panic drowned out all her words and I found myself echoing Nate, pleading in whispered tones. "I'll never use it—I swear! Just don't say anything!"

A soft hand clamped over my mouth as she stared reassuringly into my eyes. "Jamie, I'm the *last* person who would tell."

The trembling suddenly stopped and I stared at her, remembering only then what she'd said back at the house. Her beaming confession, lost in the wake of my blind panic.

One of us.

"Did you do that on purpose?"

Her face froze at my sudden shift in tone.

"Did I do what on purpose?"

I dropped her hands, staring at her with something close to dread. "*Fall.* Did you *fall* on purpose?"

There was a horrible pause.

"Yes."

I took a step back, really seeing her for the first time. "You..."

She reached for me, those beautiful eyes swimming with tears. "But Jamie, it isn't what you think. You needed to—"

I wrenched myself free, stumbling backwards into the dark. "Just stay away from me!"

A second later, I was running again. Only this time, I did what I should have done instead of going up to that roof. I raced back to my house and shut the door, locking it firmly behind me. The stairs were just a blur, then I was barricading myself in my room, yanking the curtains over my window for good measure and climbing into bed with the comforter pulled up to my eyes.

Only then, alone in the darkness, did I let myself cry.

BY THE NEXT MORNING, I'd almost convinced myself I imagined it. Almost convinced myself it was all a dream. If it wasn't for the fact that I was still wearing grass-covered sneakers, I might've believed myself. I kicked them off with a shiver, and then forced myself to breathe deep.

This was not the end. I simply wouldn't allow it. No one else on the planet knew my secret. Only Gabby. And if she told mine, then I'd tell hers. Mutually assured destruction.

I pulled in another breath, completely confident this wouldn't happen.

No—I was safe. I was safe, and this was under control, and everything was going to continue just the way it had been the day before. I just had to act normal.

And stay away from pencils.

And avoid the roof at all costs.

I can do that.

Armed with fresh determination, I dressed quickly and headed downstairs to find something to eat. Sunlight was streaming in through the shuttered windows and my father was nowhere in sight. I decided to take both as a sign. A very good sign.

No reason this couldn't be a normal day.

I grabbed an apple off the counter, vowing to embrace every teenage normalcy on the spot. Maybe after school I'd waste some time on social media. Then I could spend the rest of the afternoon texting girls and contemplating a tattoo. By the time I'd poured myself a glass of juice, I was seriously considering contacting Kevin McConnell about buying some pot.

That's when I saw them.

Men in bulletproof vests.

On the grass cutting across to my house. Then pouring in from both sides of the kitchen.

There had to be at least twenty, crowding out the sunlight in a tide of Kevlar and steel. I remember briefly thinking they looked like ants. Scuttling in uniform formation under their black helmets. Their shoes scuffed the tile. One of them knocked over a vase.

The juice was still in my hand. I set it down slowly. I didn't understand why they were moving so strangely, aggressively. Fencing me in. It didn't strike me until later that they were used to having kids try to run. A radio crackled and I jumped a mile, staring with wide saucer eyes.

"James Hunt?"

I couldn't speak. I simply nodded.

Then a suited man in the front came towards me. "Don't move."

"Dad?" I backed away to the wall, calling out reflexively toward the hallway.

Two more men grabbed me just as the front door opened and shut. My voice rose in panic as they pressed me into the cabinets, holding out my arms.

"Dad! Please! Help me!"

And then he was there. Standing right in front of me.

The men holding me vanished and my mouth fell open in shock. I'd never seen him move that fast. I didn't think I'd seen anyone move that fast. Not in real life.

"Not my son."

The words scalded the air and the men with armored vests and guns fell back a step, wilting under his gaze like frightened school children.

Only one of them dared speak. The same one who had asked my name. "But sir, we have orders to—"

"Not. My. Son."

That was it. As quickly as it started, the assault was over.

The men cleared out of our house faster than you would believe. Saying not a word as they swept past the picture frames and over the pristine rugs. One of them mumbled some sort of apology about the vase, but a single look at my father's face was enough to quiet him. He disappeared like all the rest, piling into white vans before racing away.

The front door slammed shut behind them. Leaving a deafening silence in their wake.

I hadn't moved more than a few feet since it happened. I went just far enough to leave the kitchen and make sure they had actually gone. Strangely enough, my father stayed right beside me.

Stranger still—he'd kept a hand on me the entire time.

I don't think he realized it himself. It wasn't until I fidgeted, trapped at a weird angle, that he seemed to notice I was there. His eyes snapped up and he released me all in the same moment, looking as close to uncomfortable as I had ever seen.

"Are you all right?" he asked.

It was brusque. Almost cold. The same tone I'd used with Gabby just the night before, when I so desperately wanted to make sure that she was okay.

"Yeah, I'm fine." I straightened my clothes, trying not to act as shaken as I felt. "What just...what were those guys doing here?"

My father's eyes gleamed as they fixed on the door, chilling the room with an expression I knew would haunt my dreams from here on out. "I'm not sure. But you can bet I'm going to find out."

With that, he set out across the floor—assumedly to chase down those vans on foot and rip them to pieces. It wasn't until he reached the front door that he paused. "James, they didn't..."

He faltered for the first time, casting a fleeting glance over his shoulder. Our eyes met and I shook my head slowly, answering the question he couldn't bring himself to say.

They never got a sample.

He nodded curtly and left without another word. Keys in hand. Pure hell burning in his eyes.

It wasn't until he was gone that I realized what a close call it had actually been. What the men would have found if they'd succeeded in testing my DNA. A belated shiver ran down my arms and I sucked in a sudden breath, feeling like I'd dodged a high-caliber bullet.

I dropped my hands to my knees and bent over to try and stop my heart from racing.

That's when I saw the manila folder lying on the floor.

IT MUST HAVE SLIPPED out of his briefcase in the rush to get inside. That's the only explanation I could come up with. Otherwise, there was no way my father would be so careless with such a document. Eighteen years the two of us had been living together, and I had never seen a single piece of paper from his work. The man compartmentalized like a champion.

And yet...here we were.

I sat on one side of the table. The folder sat on the other.

Neither of us moved and neither of us blinked. It could have been minutes or hours later—I no longer had any sense of time. My mind was completely centered on this one solitary thing.

It wasn't sealed, I could see that much. In fact, if I tilted my head just so I could see the faint trace of lettering scribbled up the side. Every time the fan blew, the edges fluttered open.

Leave it alone. Just walk away.

If I were being smart, I would have listened to my own advice. If I were thinking clearly, I wouldn't have picked it up in the first place. But I wasn't being smart. I wasn't thinking clearly.

The assault team in the kitchen had been a wake-up call I wasn't ready for. It was a not-so-subtle reminder that this... *situation* of mine couldn't be swept under the rug by the power of positive thought. No amount of lip-piercing, or curfew-breaking, or other teenage hyphenates was going to force things back to normal. There were people interested in what I was. Men with guns and itchy trigger fingers.

And I didn't want to hear it. I wasn't emotionally prepared to think about it. I was still having a panic attack every time I looked down at my hands. I had been left here with the juice, and the broken vase, and this file...and I was going to freaking-well see what was inside.

Even if it was very, *very* stupid for me to do so.

Before I could succumb to my wiser angels, I snatched the folder off the table and threw open the top page. It wasn't what I expected. No black-and-white mug shots, Cyrillic writing, or redacted text for me to puzzle through. There was just a single slip of paper. It was a list of names.

Written in my father's slanted hand.

What the—?

As I leaned forward to examine it closer, a second paper fell out. It had been taped just below the first, and had been printed so lightly it was almost hard to read.

This one was all numbers. Credit card numbers. Social security numbers. Cell phone numbers. Each one corresponding with a name on the list. And there was something else as well.

The person's age.

I leaned back in my chair, breathing hard, looking at the first name on the list.

Ruby Walker. Age fifteen. No real credit history, but she had a cell phone. Every kid in America had a cell phone. This one listed her as living somewhere in New York.

My heart rate spiked. There was a hitch in my breathing.

They were coming for Ruby Walker—my father and his men. It didn't matter that she was a child. It didn't matter that she hadn't done anything wrong. They were going to show up at her house, or at her school, or in the middle of her soccer practice and shove her into a van.

There would be no trial. No lawyer. No chance to appeal. All records would be sealed, and little Ruby Walker, instead of worrying about whether the boy in homeroom was going to ask her to the prom, was going to end up in a governmental black hole.

She'd die there. They all died there. It was only a matter of time.

The paper twisted in my hands—the one with the numbers. I had no idea if or when my father was coming home. I had no idea if he knew he'd even lost the file. But time was running out. For me and for Ruby Walker and all the other names on this list I held in my hands. Whatever was going to happen had to happen now.

I reached for my phone in my back pocket and then dialed with one hand. The other was gripped hard on the table.

"Hello?"

My mouth went dry as the phone went rigid in my palm.

"Hello?" She was impatient now, probably checking the number. "Who is this?"

It's now or never. Say what you called to say.

"Ruby?" I cleared my throat and tried again. "Is this Ruby Walker?"

"Yeah..." She sounded curious. She sounded *young*. I imagined her with braids and an umbrella, tilting her head. "Who's this?"

"This is—"

I caught myself quickly. It was bad enough I was calling without revealing who I was. A car drove past the front window and I was suddenly in a rush.

"Listen, I'm going to say something terrible, but I need to you hear it all the way through, all right? I need you to *not* hang up the phone. Can you do that for me?"

There was a lengthy pause. Only her shallow breathing let me know she hadn't hung up.

"Ruby?"

"Yeah...I'm here."

I shut my eyes. Pulled in a deep breath.

"The people at Obtero know you have the gene. They're coming for you, if they're not on their way already. Wherever you are, you need to get out—do you hear me? You don't have time to get anything, you just need to leave."

A small part of myself was saying the same thing. A small part was wondering why I hadn't already packed a bag. Hopped onto the next bus. Vanished from my seaside town.

My father knows...doesn't he? My father knows I have the gene.

"Okay, who is this?!" Ruby was angry now. Her trilling voice panicked to rage. "Is this supposed to be funny? Some kind of sick joke—"

"We both know I'm not wrong." My fingers tightened on the phone, suddenly desperate for this stranger I would never see to believe me. "Why would I lie?"

There was another pause. A much longer one this time; I could almost hear the wheels spinning as she thought through what I just told her. Then she said just a single word.

"Thanks."

The line went dead.

All the air rushed out of my chest as I leaned back in my chair. Feeling like I'd just run a gauntlet. Staring down at my trembling hands. My pulse was skyrocketing, and even if you gave me a thousand years I'd never be able to believe what I had just done.

Then I picked up the phone and did it again.

And again. And again.

Chapter 13

My father didn't come home that night. It was kind of an unspoken assumption that I wouldn't go to school. I had no intention of going the next day either. Or the one after that really.

What would I do? Camp out in fourth period and wait for the assault team? Bide my time in physics until they got their sample and hauled me out in chains?

Not. My. Son.

That was all well and good in our kitchen, but how far did it stretch?

My father was supposed to be one of the only people in the world who had the power to make that call. To make the rules and make things off limits. To make them back off.

Then what the heck happened this morning?!

Those men were acting on orders. Following a mission statement my own father knew nothing about. How was that possible? Who in the world had both the nerve and authority to supersede Alexander Hunt in his own company? I wasn't going to be at school when I found out.

I wasn't going to be in the same time zone.

For the second time that day, I found myself standing on forbidden ground. Staring at things that weren't mine.

Do it.

The row of sports cars gleamed under the fluorescent lights. Fast, even in stillness. Since I was thirteen, they had each claimed a small piece of my heart.

Just take one.

Wasn't that internal voice of mine supposed to be a caution? Little whispers of wisdom to balance out all those reckless impulses? Like an adolescent early warning system?

...doesn't apply to cars.

The keys twisted in my hand. It had been a big step just to take them off the hook. In eighteen years I had never been so bold. The sin was committed. Just one thing left to do...

Screw it.

I took the Swedish one. The one I could never pronounce. My hands were moving quickly, but it was still with the utmost care that I pulled open the door and slid inside. A forbidden aroma washed over my face. The decadent aroma of leather, the gleam of the chrome, and everything teenage dreams are made of. If I had the talent, I would write songs about this car. But there wasn't time. Maybe later. Right now I had to leave.

With a shaking hand I pressed the button to open the garage door, and then tossed the control out the window onto the floor. I wouldn't need it again. I wouldn't be coming back. The keys slid into the ignition, and with a grace and power I attributed to things like dragons the car sailed onto the open driveway. Responding to my slightest touch. The sound of the engine thrumming throughout the vehicle with a quiet purr.

It was orange. But I could forgive that for its speed. And I needed speed now. Wherever I was going, I figured I wouldn't have that much of a head start.

I paused just a moment in the street right in front of my house. Just long enough to decide which way to turn the wheel. Just long enough to cast a secret glance at the house next door.

Then I shot to the left. Away from the ocean. Towards the middle of the United States.

Enjoy it. Enjoy the freedom while you can.

IT WASN'T A SHOCK TO realize that I hadn't exactly thought my great escape through.

I'd gotten the idea in the shower, trying to calm down after my series of damning international rescue calls. Calls I'd made from my own cell phone—in case there was any doubt as to fault or blame. It had been an impulse decision. Just like the one to warn Ruby Walker.

I had the gene—no time to process that.

There was a chance my father knew—an even more terrifying prospect.

Obtero was coming to Seranto High to perform 'random' sampling.

That required immediate action.

Hence the grand larceny. Hence the escape attempt. I couldn't be there when it happened. I couldn't sit at home—where they had already found me—and wait for it to happen again. I couldn't talk to my father, on the off chance he *didn't* know. And I couldn't stand to think about what he might choose to do if he did. There was only one option left.

To leave. To run away and never come back.

I imagined the fallout with the windows rolled down. Even this far away from the ocean, I could still smell the salty breeze.

My father would probably guess why I'd left. Even if he didn't know for sure, my sudden exodus would confirm his suspicions. That meant that the immediate aftermath would really be up to him. An open narrative for him to shape as he saw fit.

Knowing him as well as I did, it wasn't hard to guess what he'd do.

His son was travelling abroad—that's what he'd say. In an act of impromptu parenthood, he'd granted me a gap year before university. (How ironic that had been my dream all along.) No questions would be asked. Even if they were, they would all be dismissed with a simple:

It's James *Hunt*.

No one would question my last name. Rather, no one would question my father's last name. It was an impenetrable shield. One that had saved me from the chopping block today. And one that would continue to protect me long after I had fled this quiet seaside town.

Except that they came to YOUR house, Hunt. They were in YOUR kitchen.

Damn that voice. It could be either for me or against me. It had to make up its mind.

Yes, they came to MY house. Invaded MY kitchen. And while I was incapable of delving too deeply into that, my mind had already come up with a rational explanation. One that would staunch the bleeding and save me from further thought.

It was the pilot program.

The whole point of the program was to 'lead by example'. Obtero had chosen Seranto High—where the commandant's son was currently a senior—for that very reason. Wouldn't it make sense that said commandant's son would be the very first to be tested?

But you WEREN'T tested...

I shut the voice out entirely. It was the reason I had stolen a car.

I DROVE ALL NIGHT AND into the next day. The sun was already high overhead before I realized that I hadn't eaten since two nights before. My stomach lurched just as I pulled into a Taco Bell drive-through, checking the glove compartment to see if there was any cash.

Eating in the car. Even so far away from all those rules, I felt like I'd be lynched.

"Hello, can I take your..." The voice crackled into silence almost as quickly as it had started to speak. I stared at the box curiously. There was a brief pause, followed by a sudden exclamation. "Actually, can you just pull forward?"

My hands froze on the wheel. In my mind, every fast food joint and 7Eleven had suddenly transformed into a post office wall. Wanted posters hanging up everywhere. My face plastered at a million different angles. For all I knew, there was already a hotline set up for anonymous tips.

"I...uh..." I debated just gunning the engine. There was no one ahead of me in line. "I just wanted to order some food..."

"Yeah, absolutely!" the voice exclaimed. There were others now in the background, talking excitedly. "Just pull forward, I'll take the order."

Another pause. The car was idling restlessly. Then the window slid open and the smell of processed salt and cheese wafted over my face.

You are worst fugitive of all time.

I was being paranoid. This was the middle of nowhere. This was some tiny desert town in Northern Arizona. More like a glorified rest stop. Chances were, it wasn't even on the map.

"Yeah...okay."

I can't believe I got brought down by a freakin' taco.

With a repentant kind of caution I inched the car around the corner, leaning forward in my seat to peer inside the window. No fewer than four faces stared back at me—eyes as wide as saucers, faces crammed into the frame. But it wasn't me they were looking at.

Of course, I slumped down with a sigh of relief. *The car.*

"Dude!" The cashier started talking even before I'd pulled all the way to the window. He and two friends were already leaning outside. "That car's *insane*!"

"Thanks." I smiled weakly, trying not to think of how much trouble this insane car was going to bring down on my head. "Can I get—"

"How much did something like that run you?"

The assistant manager was speaking now. He was only a year or so older than the others, but was clearly an authority on the subject of Gran Turismo cars.

Just get out of here, Jamie. You're ON THE RUN.

"Graduation gift," I replied hurriedly, incurring the eternal wrath of all four men. They were probably going to spit in my over-privileged food. "Can I get some tacos?"

A collective shadow darkened their faces as all but one disappeared.

"Yeah, of course." He rang up my order and stuffed the bag with sauce, shooting covert glances out the window the whole time. It wasn't until I was about to drive away that he asked for a selfie.

He was holding my drink hostage. I reluctantly agreed.

My face turned instinctively to the side as the phone flashed; I was gone before he had a chance to ogle the picture. Not the most discreet encounter, but what did I expect? I was in the middle of an Arizona desert driving a two-million-dollar car.

I pulled over at the next rest stop to eat. After blanketing my legs with a thick layer of napkins, I decided it still wasn't enough and simply sat down on the pavement instead. There wasn't a person in sight. Not a single structure. Just hard, flat earth as far as the eye could see.

Maybe that's what gave me the idea...

I took a slurp of my drink, then stared down at my hands. They looked perfectly normal. Nothing at all to indicate that they could throw off sparks or light random writing implements on fire. Another slurp of soda. Everything was fine. No chance at all that I could—

With lightning speed, I threw both hands into the void. Flexing my fingers with all my strength. I'm ashamed to say there might have been some soft sound effects as well.

Nothing happened.

Encouraged and disappointed at the same time, I tried again and again. Nothing at all happened. Not a single spark, or flame, or...

Truth be told, I wasn't sure what exactly these abilities of mine were.

They were never specific on the news about just what mysterious powers the government was confiscating. We were flat-out forbidden from asking questions, and I realized for the first time that I had nothing to fall back on but my own conjectures. No real idea what I could do.

I lowered my arms to my sides, feeling a little foolish. As the sun beat down on me, scorching the tops of my cheeks, I made a mental list.

Flames. Sparks. Speed. Strength.

Ability to survive an attack by a three-hundred-pound linebacker.

There was no common thread. Nothing except 'beyond the ordinary' to tie all of these traits together. Over the years, I'd successfully trained myself to stop thinking about those people who had the gene. After being force-fed the party line for so long, I ceased to be jealous and actually began to view it as a liability. Having the gene was like having a black spot hovering over their heads and marking them for recovery.

When I *had* bothered to think about it—back when I was a child and the idea of the supernatural filled my drawings and dreams—I'd only ever imagined people having just one. A specific gift that was tailor-made to their personality. Sneaky people would be able to camouflage like chameleons. People who lived near the ocean could control water. The bravest would be strong.

Thinking about it now, I realized how stupid that was. These gifts were a biological quirk not an existential extension. And when had I started calling them gifts again, instead of abilities?

So then, what? I'm just...enhanced?

I glanced over my shoulder at the tiny restroom. Crumbling plaster with weeds sprouting through the cracks. Then without any warning, I sprinted towards it as fast as I could.

...and reached it a few seconds later.

Nothing enhanced about that.

Feeling like more and more of an idiot, I tried everything I could think of. Racing around the parking lot. Setting my trash on fire. At one point, I even tried lifting the car.

Nothing.

If there was a drone up there watching me, whoever was at the controls was having a laugh. I paused suddenly and amended the thought with a shiver. If there was a drone up there watching, I had bigger problems then my spark-free hands.

"Well, that's just perfect," I muttered, walking dejectedly back to the car. "The only silver lining in this mess and I can't even get it to—"

A shower of sparks shot out of my hands just as I was reaching for the door.

"Crap—No! I'm so sorry!"

My hands clasped over my mouth as I stared in horror as the scorched paint. A second later I remembered what those hands had just done and stretched them as far away from my face as possible, aiming my palms at the ground.

Did you actually just apologize to the car?

"Did I actually just..." I tried to silence the voice with more pressing matters, but found that I didn't have the air. "My hands, how did that..."

With a broken breath, I sank to my knees.

"...what's happening to me?"

I should have been afraid. I should have been bitter. If I was being honest, I also should have secretly been a little excited. But I was none of those things. What I was, however, surprised me.

I was sad. Desperately, hopelessly sad.

This was real. My life was really over. There was no way to ignore it or wish it away. I had just shot sparks out of my hands. I was one of *those* people now. The people who had numbers, not names. The people you saw on the news and quickly switched the channel with a shudder There was only so long I could keep it under wraps. It was only a matter of time before I ended up in one of those vans.

Just eighteen years old, but I'd never get the chance to do anything. To live my life, go to college, fall in love. All that was going to be taken away. And it was probably going to be taken by the one person who should have loved me and protected me over all.

Get up, Jamie. Get in the car.

There was someone else coming. Probably a few miles away, but I could already see the dust coming up from their tires. The last thing I needed was another paint-scorched selfie.

With a shuddering breath, I got to my feet and threw away my trash. A second later I was pulling back onto the interstate, aiming east. What I hoped to find there, I had no idea. When I planned to stop, I didn't know. For now, the plan was simple.

Keep driving. Keep driving until I ran out of road.

Then I planned to walk. Or swim. Or whatever it took.

A SHARP BUMP JOLTED me in my sleep. A piercing screech, and my eyes snapped open.

"Crap!"

My foot slammed on the brakes as I angled my entire body against the wheel, trying desperately to wrench the car away from the center divider. A second later I went spiraling out to freedom, only to lurch to a stop on the side of the road.

That's when I saw the lights. And heard the sirens.

"Crap, crap, crap!"

Every drop of color vanished from my face as I twisted around in my seat, staring with wide eyes through the back window. It flashed alternating shades of blue and red, and even though we were the only two cars on the road that shrill siren had yet to stop screeching.

What am I supposed to do?

I called out into the void as the cop climbed from his vehicle. No reply. For better or worse, I was on my own. In the middle of the desert. In what had to look like a stolen car.

Should I turn myself in?

No. Absolutely not. Next idea.

Should I drive off?

The idea seemed ridiculous—they *shot* at people fleeing the police. And yet, we were the only people for miles. This car was built for speed. The ground was flat; I could wait until I lost him, turn off the headlights, and circle back around. By the time he and the others figured it out, I could already be a hundred miles away—

"Roll down the window, son."

Shit.

My mouth went dry, but my palms were sweating as I hurried to do as he asked. It didn't help my cause that it took a few seconds to find the right button. The car was like a space ship with all the buttons and switches.

At first the cop was visibly surprised by my age. He remembered his script a second later.

"Do you know why I pulled you over tonight?"

If you're asked a direct question, it's best to give a direct answer. Volunteer as much of the truth as you can. I remembered my father telling me that.

"I fell asleep." My hands were clenched on the wheel, knuckles white.. "I'm sorry, I-I didn't realize how late it was."

How late was it? And where the hell was I? Was it possible I was still in Arizona, or did this officer hail from somewhere in the Bible Belt?

The cop nodded slowly, then lifted his flashlight—shining it in my eyes. "Have you been drinking, son?"

I shook my head with a wince, temporarily blinded. "Only a soda."

I should have kept it as evidence, just in case I was asked. He seemed somehow amused by my answer—the mustache twitched up at the corners. But that faded when he saw the car.

"Can I see your license and registration?"

Crap! I should have run.

"Actually...this is my dad's car." I handed him my license anyway, cursing the gods that I couldn't think of anything better to do. "He let me borrow it for the night."

The cop let out a slow whistle, staring from bumper to bumper. "What's your dad—a king or something?"

Kind of. Depends who you ask.

I just flashed a tight smile, drumming my fingers nervously on the wheel. After a few seconds of silence, I ventured the question. "Is that a crime? Falling asleep at the wheel?"

His eyes shot up, but one look at my face softened him. Marginally.

"Kind of. Depends who you ask."

Had I really just said that out loud?

"Some people might let you off with a warning," he continued in a slow drawl. "Others see it as negligent homicide. You're straddling state lines, so it's hard to get a consensus."

I gulped hard, nodding quickly. "Which one am I closer to?"

Again, he seemed to find this funny. Again, he was sobered by the sight of such an expensive car.

"You may be telling the truth or you may not. Now I can see here that you're eighteen, so I'll tell you what. You want to avoid a ticket? A quick call to your father will clear it right up."

My face whitened as I froze dead still. "...my father?"

"You said he lent you the car, right?" the cop interrupted, a lot sharper than his slow speech would have led me to believe. "Let me hear that from him and you're off the hook."

"He, uh...the thing is—"

"Kid, you've got one chance here."

"I'll take the ticket," I blurted.

Wrong answer.

The flashlight was back. This time, there wasn't a hint of a smile.

"Step out of the car. Hands on the hood."

I cringed in my seat, breathing so hard I thought I might pass out. "But you said—"

"*Step out of the car.*" One hand went to his belt, resting on all the little toys that were hanging there. "*Hands on the hood.*"

I couldn't tell if I was nodding or shaking. Either way, I did as he asked. Keeping both hands in plain sight I stepped onto the pavement, praying they wouldn't spontaneously light themselves on fire. The night air was freezing; I found myself wishing I'd remembered a jacket as I placed both palms on the car, feeling like a B-movie criminal.

The cop was saying something into his radio. My ears were ringing too loud for me to hear a word. For a split second, I considered taking off on foot.

Then he let out a sudden gasp. "Hunt?" He held up my license again, really looking at it for the first time. "Your name is James Hunt? As in..." He trailed off into silence, mentally filling in the rest. Twice, his eyes travelled from my face to the car. Three times. A second later, he was convinced. "Well, I'll be."

I jumped a mile as he let out a loud whoop, slapping his knee for good measure.

Definitely somewhere in the Bible Belt.

"I can see now why you didn't want me calling!" He laughed again, wiping actual tears from his face. "Taking Daddy's car for a little joyride?"

I bit back my automatic reply, bowing my head and forcing myself to look respectful. If there was one thing 'Daddy' had taught me, it was when to hold my tongue.

Instead I gave him a tentative smile, cocking my head towards the car. "What would you do?"

The cop laughed again, lowering the flashlight now that we were on the same side.

"Yeah, I could see that being a bit of a temptation." He couldn't stop chuckling, thrilled with his luck. "What was the plan? Sneak it out after dark, have it back by sunrise?"

"Yeah...something like that." I played along and tried to keep calm. If anything this exonerated me, right? He knew it was a family car, not stolen. "So...can I go?" I flashed another coaxing smile, hating myself for it all the while. "If I promise not to drive it off the road?"

For a second, I thought it had worked. For a second, I thought he would let me.

I should have known better.

"Listen, James, I hate to say it, but—" His face lightened suddenly. "Actually, it's Jamie, right? I think I read that somewhere."

I bit the inside of my cheek, trying not to lose my temper. "It's Jamie."

"Well, Jamie, I hate to say it, but...*Alexander Hunt*?" He stressed the name like I was supposed to be impressed, like I was supposed to understand. "The chance to return his prized car? Not to mention his *son*?" He chuckled again. "No, kid. I'm afraid you're coming with me."

My shoulders slumped and I dropped my hands with a sigh. This was it, then. I was screwed. Just a few hours later, I'd be back in my living room. That is, if I was lucky.

While the cop called in a tow, I trudged to the back of the squad car. I was just pulling open the door, when he rushed forward to stop me.

"Oh no, son—it's fine. You can ride up front with me."

Seriously?

I had a much harder time keeping my emotions off my face as I slid into the passenger seat, but the officer didn't seem to notice. He was already texting all his friends, one foot bouncing excitedly as he fired up the engine. I was just waiting for a repeat of the selfie.

Silver lining, at least I was no longer worried he was going to Tase me.

That being said, I had no idea what I might end up accidentally doing to him.

THIS HAS GOT TO BE rock bottom.

The cop might have let me ride shotgun. He even offered to buy me a coffee as we passed an all-night drive-through on the way into town. But the second we rolled to a stop in the parking lot, he was all business once again.

There was a small crowd waiting and the man had been born to entertain.

He led me into the precinct, slowly. One hand firmly on my shoulder, the other firmly on his belt. Once we were inside, he actually waited for the crowd to catch up before sauntering up to the front desk and announcing the name of his prisoner.

James *Hunt*. Yes—that's the one.

It took everything I had in me not to roll my eyes.

After giving me a bizarre tour of the facility and explaining all kinds of unnecessary crime statistics I would never need to know, he sat me down and lectured for ten minutes on the importance of being a responsible driver. He also touched on the importance of staying awake at the wheel. And the importance of respecting one's elders. I could have sworn he actually looked vaguely apologetic at the last part, but his friends were watching, and there was a chance the great Alexander Hunt would hear about it himself. When he was finished, he led me to a holding cell.

That stopped me cold.

"Uh...really?"

I couldn't tell you exactly what it was, but something about seeing that iron door slowly swing open filled me with an unspeakable feeling of dread.

His eyes flickered back to the other officers before he lowered his voice. "I'm sorry, kid, but it's the rule. If it was just us I'd let you wait in my office, but—"

"Let me wait in the office," I blurted, followed by a much milder, "please." There was a pause and I lowered my voice as well, giving him every opportunity to save face. "You said it yourself, I didn't commit any crime. *Please*. Let me wait in the office."

We locked eyes and he'd actually started to nod, when a voice called out from the back. "What's the holdup, Jim? The kid trying to bribe you with his car?"

And that was the end of the office.

Four hours later I was sitting on the floor, having bypassed the questionable looking mattress. Wrists cuffed and dangling over my knees. Wondering vaguely what would happen when I inevitably needed to use the bathroom.

This is rock bottom.

A noise at the other end of the hall caught my attention. It had been quiet for hours, long enough for the slightest sound to make me jump. There was a faint jingling of keys, followed by a distant sound of conversation. A moment later, Officer Jim was headed my way.

"Looks like it's your lucky night."

That's one way of looking at it.

"Oh yeah?" I pushed stiffly to my feet. "How's that?"

He unlocked the door to my cell, smiling.

"It seems you already had some people out looking for you. When we put out the alert, one of them called almost immediately. He's here now to pick you up."

THIS is rock— No, I've got to stop saying it!

"Oh yeah?" I said again. There was a tremor in my voice I couldn't hide. One that somehow jumped into my hands as my eyes locked on the end of the corridor. "Who's that?"

Jim's eyes twinkled as the door opened again.

"You'll know him. I recognized him myself from TV."

Time seemed to slow down as I stood there with bated breath. The hallway seemed to lengthen fifty feet. For a moment, all was quiet. Then a tall man strode underneath the lights.

It could have been worse. It could have been a lot worse.

"Uncle Jake?"

Chapter 14

Jacob Hennessey wasn't technically my uncle, but ever since I was five years old I'd addressed him as such. The man had been to every tee-ball game. Every disastrous school play I'd taken part in. He'd flown in from Greece just to attend my junior high graduation. When high school started the attendance slowed, but he was a busy man.

Jake was my father's business partner, turned second-in-command. They'd started Obtero in their twenties; conceived it in my grandparents' basement and launched it from in an empty warehouse on the Brooklyn waterfront. Brooklyn quickly turned to Manhattan. The government contracts were soon to follow.

More importantly, Jacob Hennessey was a third option I'd never considered.

The man could be reasonable. He had long ago earned my trust.

"Permission to speak with the prisoner." His eyes twinkled as they caught mine through the bars. "Unless you think we should have him drawn and quartered right here."

I stepped forward with a wry smile as Jim laughed nervously. He was clearly uncertain how to interact with such a powerful man. Especially with his 'nephew' standing locked up in a cage.

"Would you like some coffee, sir?"

"Just the keys." Jake kept his eyes on me the entire time, holding out an expectant hand.

Jim hesitated only a moment, and then dropped them into his palm. "Like I said on the phone, I pulled him over for driving erratically—"

"What about you, kid? You want some coffee?"

The officer fell silent, then turned to look at me as well. I shook my head. The initial relief at seeing Jake had faded, and for the first time in my life I was regarding my uncle with a stab of fear. He might care for me, but he was a company man through and through.

There was a chance we were on opposite sides.

"Some privacy, then." Jake glanced at Jim for the first time as he stepped forward and slid the key into the lock. "It'll give you a chance to round up the security feed for the last six hours."

Again, the officer hesitated. Then he disappeared with a curt nod, leaving the two of us alone. By the time the door swung shut behind him, I almost wished he'd stayed.

"I hope you didn't touch that mattress."

My eyes snapped up as Jake pulled open the door, joining me inside the cell. A second later, they travelled back to the makeshift cot. I'd been awake for thirty hours. I tried to keep up.

"Do what?"

He gestured to the gruesome stains with a grin. "I'm fresh out of penicillin."

When I was too nervous to react, he took a step back—staring with a steady gaze. A second later he sat down on the floor, motioning for me to join him.

It was quiet for a few minutes, then he cast me a sideways glance.

"You want to tell me what happened?"

He doesn't know?

I gave him a fleeting look, and then dropped my eyes to the floor—shaking my head. He stared another moment, then nodded. It was quiet a few minutes more.

"How did you find me?" I asked suddenly.

It couldn't have been hard. The man sat at the head of an international intelligence agency. But, as it turned out, I'd made it even easier than all that.

"I recognized the car from the APB."

Of course he did. Why didn't I just run away in a Volvo like everyone else?

"Nice choice. The Koenigsegg?"

I kept my eyes on the floor, feeling suddenly dizzy. "Oh, is that how you say it?"

He looked at me again, then clapped a hand on my leg. "Relax, Jamie." His lips twitched as he gestured around the dank little cell. "We've all been here. Trust me."

Jake was the same age as my dad, early forties, but he'd always seemed younger. Perhaps it was the messy hair and careless smile. Perhaps it was because he didn't carry the weight of a company on his shoulders—there were fewer stress lines on his face.

I stared at him cautiously, seeing my own face reflected in those sparkling blue eyes.

Is it really possible he doesn't know?

After a moment of silence, I simply nodded. It was impossible not to feel at least a little reassured by his presence, as counterintuitive as that was. By the time the door opened again, I'd even managed a tentative smile.

"You've been here?" I repeated with a wry grin, accepting a helping hand to my feet.

"Oh, yeah—couple of times." He winked at me, but lingered a moment on my wrists. The look cooled significantly as Jim joined us with the tape. "Cuffs?"

The officer visibly deflated. I smirked behind the bars of my cage.

"Yes, well I..." He stammered and flailed beneath the weight of my uncle's stare. "Under the circumstances, I thought it best to..."

Jake nodded slowly. The smile was nothing short of terrifying.

"Jamie—go wait in my car."

I did as I was told, lifting the key off Jim's belt in the process. We locked eyes ever so briefly and I couldn't resist a tiny grin—brave, now that I was no longer alone. "Good luck."

Jake smiled indulgently, while Jim blanched with dread. I left them to it, breezing past the other officers and making it all the way to the parking lot before I heard the screams.

We might have been in the middle of the desert, but the night air was freezing cold. I dug my hands into my pockets with a shiver, wishing again for a jacket as I looked around for my uncle's car. It wasn't hard to find. He and my father shared a certain flair for the extreme.

Which meant driving something...utterly ridiculous.

A four-million-dollar Bugatti and he left it unlocked. Of course he did. Because who in their right mind would be stupid enough to consider stealing this car?

I considered it.

As I slid into the passenger seat, I thought about how easy it would be for me to make off with it into the night. Jake was surely going to be busy for another few minutes, dismembering the rest this small-town police force. That would give me at least a little head start.

He'd think it was funny. Well, maybe not. But he wouldn't be mad. When I'd crashed his Formula 310 speedboat on my thirteenth birthday, he'd led the beach in a round of applause.

My shoulders fell with a sigh as I leaned back into the headrest.

Who was I kidding? I hadn't made it forty-eight hours on my own before I managed to get picked up by the most mediocre police officer this side of the Mississippi. Did I really think I stood a chance of slipping away into the night in Jacob Hennessey's car?

Speak of the devil.

"Sorry for the wait." My uncle slid into the car with a cheerful smile, tossing me a flash of silver in the process. "Just doing a little restructuring."

I stared at him curiously, glancing down at my hands. It was a badge for the Winslow Police Force, formally belonging to Officer Jim Millstone. Now just a souvenir.

I ran my fingers along the edges, then tossed it out the window. "What's going to happen to the car?"

"What car?" he asked distractedly, rifling around in the backseat.

"My dad's car. The..." I didn't even try to pronounce it. The poor thing was sitting on the bed of a tow truck on the other side of the lot. "Shouldn't I be driving it back?"

For a moment, we both stared at it. Mourning a fallen giant.

"No...my guess is you don't want your dad to see it looking like that." My whole body wilted and Jake chuckled under his breath. "Don't worry, I'll have it fixed up and shipped back to your house. In the meantime, I can give you a ride home."

A ride home. Like I'd been stranded at the local Starbucks instead of recovered from a police station somewhere on Interstate 40.

"...thanks." My voice came out soft but sincere. And resigned. In the last few minutes, the dark reality of my situation had settled over me like a cloud. In all likelihood, this would be the last time I was travelling freely over state lines. Might as well get used to the idea.

He cast me a look, then forced a bit of levity. "So...where to, kid?"

I flashed a smile in spite of myself.

It was our inside joke. A question he'd asked me since I was just a child. Over the years, I'd answered in different ways. At first, it was places like Disneyland and Coney Island. As I got older it turned into Ibiza and Cancun. He always took me. No matter what I said. He'd simply nod, point with a frown in the general direction, then fire up the engine.

"How about Australia?" he prompted. "Great surfing this time of year."

The smile froze painfully on my face. It was a kind effort, but it wasn't fooling anyone. We both knew exactly where I was going. And exactly who'd be waiting for me to arrive.

"That sounds great," I replied, with as much enthusiasm as I could muster. "Really great."

For the first time his smile faltered, and he stifled a quiet sigh. A second later, he handed me a jacket he'd recovered from the backseat.

"Get some sleep, Jamie. You've had a long day."

Sure. Sleep. There was NO WAY that was happening.
Thirty seconds later, I blacked out.

I PASSED OUT IN ARIZONA and woke up the next day in Southern California—my forehead pressed against the window, a second jacket pillowed beneath my head. Jake was still driving, drumming his fingers absentmindedly on the wheel. He glanced over with a smile the second I blinked open my eyes and handed me a bagel. There was a coffee in the center console.

Despite having driven through the night, the man looked impossibly refreshed. Just like my father, he seemed to require very little sleep. I was a slightly different story.

"Where are we?" I asked in a gravelly voice.

"Funny you should ask," he answered brightly. "We just passed the charming little town of Lonsmith. I was considering making a detour so we could see a ten-foot block of cheese..."

I snorted under my breath, pulling off a piece of bagel. "Are we that hard-pressed for entertainment? Did you then remember we'd need a twenty-foot cracker as well?"

"Well, it was either that or buying you a one-way ticket to Iceland."

My head snapped up, but he kept his eyes on the road.

A one-way ticket?

I couldn't tell if he was joking. I couldn't tell if something more was being implied. That was rare—Jake and I were usually on the same page.

His visits had become more sporadic over the years, but I remembered each fondly. That was mostly because he always insisted on taking me along. He and my father didn't conduct business in the office, or corporate headquarters, or behind any other locked door. Upon Jake's request, they did it at ball games. At racetracks. Even one time at an impromptu trip to Six Flags

It was blasphemy in my father's eyes, the breach in professionalism. I loved it. Nothing was ever so important that I couldn't come along; and I was always, *always* given a seat at the table.

Tell him. Ask him for help.

The whole world seemed to suspend as I considered it.

On the one hand, there wasn't anyone better.

Jake had snuck me beer in elementary school, taken me trick-or-treating as a child. There weren't many adults in my life I could count on to show up, but Jacob Hennessey was one of them. The man had no obligation, but he genuinely cared. Aside from that he was wealthy, resourceful, and smart. If there was ever a way to drop off the grid, he could help me do it.

On the other hand...

He had literally co-founded the company to hunt down people with the gene. He and my father worked side by side together every day to achieve that goal. He'd dedicated his life to it.

Weighed against all that...I wasn't sure how much trick-or-treating mattered.

He cares about you. He watched you grow up.

I bit my lip, too frightened to say it.

If there's ever a time to take a chance...

"Jake—"

"Find us some music, kid." He flipped on the radio, flashing me a deliberately casual smile. "We're only a few hours out."

My heart sank as my eyes dropped back to the road.

A few hours out.

THE SUN WAS BEGINNING to set by the time we rounded the familiar corner onto Tressmen Street. Jake and I hadn't said much since the strange exchange when I woke up, despite having stopped for a lengthy lunch, which I spent dreaming of Iceland. When we finally rolled to a stop he cleared his throat awkwardly, idling in front of the house.

"Home, sweet home."

Jake had been there the day my parents bought the house. He, my father, and my mother had all gone to MIT together and were inseparable in those early days. At one point, I think he was considering buying the house next door. The one Gabby was living in now.

Coincidentally, MIT was one of the few top tier schools I was not considering.

Try again. Either that or you go inside.

"You know, things have been...hard lately." I spoke quickly and softly, keeping my eyes locked firmly on my hands. "A few weeks ago, everything started—"

"Your dad is trying his best, Jamie."

I looked up quickly, then dropped my eyes back to my lap. "It isn't that. It's just..."

The house loomed up just over my shoulder. I could feel it getting bigger with every word that I spoke. If I didn't get this out now, it would crush me. There'd be no coming back.

"Jake...can I talk to you for a second?"

Our eyes met in the darkness, exactly the same shade of blue. For an endless moment, the whole world seemed to stand still.

Then he looked away.

"You have nothing to worry about, kid. It was just a joyride." He spoke lightly but there was a strange intensity behind every word. "You weren't running away, right?"

'You climbed up there, right? Remember you CLIMBED up there.'

Why did adults always do that? Try so hard to turn your life narrative into their own?

There was a moment of silence, and then I slipped out of his jacket.

No," I said softly, climbing out of the car, "I wasn't running away."

He watched as I slowly made my way up the grass. Hands deep in my pockets, shivering slightly in just a t-shirt and jeans. I'd almost made it to the front porch when he rolled down the window, calling softly into the dark. "Jamie, I forgot to tell you...happy birthday."

My lips parted, but I could think of nothing to say. After a few seconds I simply nodded my head, lifting my hand in a stiff wave as the car rolled down the street.

...and turned back around at the corner.

The tires screeched against the asphalt as the ostentatious car whipped around in a circle, flying back up the road and slamming to a sudden stop right behind my father's. I froze perfectly still, watching in shock as my uncle stepped onto the driveway—sliding up his sunglasses with a smile so casual you'd never think to guess what was waiting inside.

"On second thought, I might as well say hi to your dad." He slipped an arm around my shoulders, leading me fearlessly up the walk. "Don't want him to get jealous."

I resisted the urge to hug him. I resisted the urge to cling to his coat, or sprint back to his car and beg him to drive me away. I simply nodded, leaning into his arm with a trembling smile.

"Wouldn't want that."

The door was unlocked. Like the Bugatti my father had developed an ironically lax sense of security, considering his profession. The second we stepped inside, the office door slammed shut and he came sweeping down the hallway...only to stop dead in his tracks.

"Jake..."

The rest of the sentence died on his lips and he simply stood there, staring between the two of us. Staring at the arm that connected us. Looking like he was going to be sick.

I didn't understand it. I'd expected explosive rage.

"Alex!" My uncle took over when it became clear my father couldn't speak. He kept a hand on me all the while, his body angled casually between us. "That has to be the *worst* welcome I've ever got. And that's definitely saying something, considering what we do."

It was like my father woke up. He blinked quickly, recovering himself. "What are you doing here? I wasn't expecting you."

"I was in the neighborhood," Jake explained with that same casual smile, keeping his eyes locked on my father the entire time. "Granted, I started racing towards the neighborhood when I heard about what happened. Obtero came to your home? Unsanctioned?"

Of course.

I hadn't put it together—the reason my uncle was already on the road at the time of my arrest. Why he'd been checking the police reports, how he'd contacted the station so quickly.

"Why didn't you call me?" he continued with the hint of a frown. "A level-five recovery unit? That must have scared the hell out of your kid."

The word was a trigger, and my father noticed me for the first time.

"James, I'm...I'm sorry to have taken off like that." Apologies didn't come easy to him; this one was hardly for my benefit. "Obviously there were things at work that required my immediate attention. I'm assuming...I'm assuming you haven't gone to school?"

Since Monday? Had I really avoided school since Monday?

My lips parted uncertainly.

Did he really not know I'd been gone?!

"When did you get back?" Jake inserted curiously, asking my silent question.

My father shot him a quick look, then gestured to his briefcase—which was still sitting on the floor. "Just now. Just a few minutes before you." His eyes returned to me. Only after years of experience could I detect a faint trace of panic. "James? Have you been to school?"

Snap out of it!

"No, I-I haven't been anywhere." I could have sworn Jake gave my shoulder a little squeeze. "I mean, Jake just took me out to dinner."

"You know they re-vamped the menu at Paulo's?" he added seamlessly. "Got risotto just like what we used to have in Florence. You, me, and Emily."

Emily was my mother. Her name stopped the conversation cold.

"James, go up to your room." My father's voice sent chills racing up the back of my spine. "Your uncle and I have business to discuss."

Never too important for me. Always a seat at the table.

But this time, Jake didn't stop him. He and my father were operating on a whole other playing field. Speaking in coded commonalities I didn't understand.

I backed away to the front door, moving carefully although neither was watching.

"I'll just...go for a run."

They didn't acknowledge it. I doubt they even heard. The two men only had eyes for each other. Gearing up for some kind of epic explosion. One I would avoid at all costs.

Without a backward glance, I swept back outside and sprinted down the length of my driveway. A huge part of me was tempted to keep going. To simply pick a direction and continue my hapless escape on foot. But even as I considered it, I knew it was no longer an option.

My jeep was in the driveway. My father and now my uncle had fenced it in. One was oblivious. One might have been intentional.

By some astronomical stroke of luck, my father didn't know that I'd taken off. Didn't know about the arrest. Didn't know that I'd destroyed the paint job on his sacred car. By some astronomical stroke of luck, my uncle had found me. Helped me. Stood in on my behalf.

But that luck had run its course. Jake wouldn't be so forgiving a second time. And my father didn't know the meaning of the word.

I slowed my pace to a brisk jog as I made my way down the street. I paused ever so briefly in front of the Tanners'. Cast a fleeting look at the card table propped up in place of a door. Gabrielle was no doubt prowling inside, hunting down stray raccoons.

For a second, I almost stopped. Then it all flashed back through my head.

Her falling off the roof in slow motion. Dark hair swirling up around her. Pale hands reaching up to the sky. Those huge eyes reflecting the moonlight. The taste of her lips on mine.

Did you do it on purpose?

...yes.

Bitter adrenaline burned the back of my throat and I pushed on, leaving the grove of trees behind. But as soon as I did, another memory struck me. One I hadn't understood until now.

It has EVERYTHING to do with you! How is it POSSIBLE that you still don't—

"Ow!"

With a muted cry, I tumbled to the ground. My legs suddenly giving out beneath me. Palms were scraping across the gravelly road. I couldn't explain it. It was like my body had simply stopped moving mid-stride. My forehead touched lightly against the road before I pushed slowly to my feet.

I was shaking. But it wasn't from the fall.

"Jamie!" There was the sound of a window sliding open, and the next second Gabrielle was running my way. "Are you all right? What the heck just happened?"

I turned to face her, feeling like my feet were barely touching the ground. "Gabby..."

"I know you said to leave you alone and I'm *doing* that, all right?" She took my hands with a scowl, pulling out a small piece of stone. "I only came out here because you fell down apropos of *nothing* in front of my house. There's a chance you might be insane."

"Gabby, I just—"

She tuned me out, muttering under her breath. "...look like you'd been attacked by a ghost."

I yanked back my hands, spraying the ground between us with blood. "Would you shut up for one second!"

The street went abruptly quiet. A luxury minivan turned around and drove the other way.

"It's my fault," I finished quietly, barely able to breathe. "They're here because of me."

She pulled in a quick breath, like someone had shoved her. Then her shoulders fell with a tired sigh. Yes. It was true. It had taken weeks of gentle prodding, but I finally knew it was true.

Those beautiful eyes shone with pity. All the anger faded away.

"Yeah, Jamie."

I let out a quiet breath, staring down at the road. "But how could they know?"

She took an automatic step closer, then backed away. "Anyone who saw you make that throw at the football game? The parents of that giant linebacker you held off with a single hand? It's already up on YouTube, Jamie."

I'm such an idiot. How did I ever think it would be fine?

A sudden thought seized me, throwing me into a cold sweat. "But my dad—"

"Why do you think your dad went after Nate?" she interrupted angrily. "Arrest the kid running, to distract from the kid throwing the ball." She shook her head in disgust. "He must have thought he hit the jackpot when he found out about Jessup. Son of a—"

She fell silent at the look on my face. My eyes had filled with tears.

"Maybe someone wants to take your dad out of the picture," she reasoned in a quieter voice. "Just like all those articles my parents found. Whenever Obtero hits a roadblock, that roadblock's kid ends up in the back of a white van."

Removing Alexander Hunt from the company by implicating his son. It wasn't entirely out of the question. There was just one glaring flaw.

"But my dad *is* Obtero." I shook my head, trying desperately to string together the ill-fitting pieces. "All those kids who have been captured? All those articles? Those were *his* orders. *His* commands."

She stared at me cautiously for a moment, hedging her bets. "What about those vans that pulled up outside your house two days ago? Were those your dad's orders? His commands?"

I could think of nothing to say to this.

"Four million dollars deposited to a bank in the Cayman Islands?" She glanced swiftly over her shoulder at the deserted street. "Come on, Jamie. That's *classic* blackmail."

My eyes travelled without thinking back to my house before I shook my head. "I don't know how it's possible, but I must have drastically mischaracterized our relationship. My father wouldn't pay a dime to save me. If he knew I had the gene, he'd turn me in himself."

I said it with grim confidence, but deep down I wondered if it was true. Hadn't he come between me and the tactical team? Hadn't he stepped without thinking between me and the men with the guns?

Not. My. Son.

The words were ringing through my head.

"I'm just telling you the facts." Another car swung around the corner and she pulled me off the road, hiding from sight inside those shadowy trees. "Just a few days after you slip up in public, Nate Jessup is arrested. Your dad gets a blackmail note and a recovery team shows up at your house. So maybe he didn't pay it. Maybe he didn't pay it *in time*. The only thing we know for sure is that your abilities aren't a secret. Somebody out there knows."

And my dad...he knows.

I remembered the look on his face when he rushed into the kitchen. The same look as when Jake and I had walked inside. It was the look of a man who was losing control.

"So where does that leave me?" I asked quietly.

I didn't really expect an answer. She didn't have one to give. She simply shook her head, backing away from me into her house.

"I don't know, Jamie. If I knew...I wouldn't be here myself."

I DON'T KNOW HOW LONG I stood there, idling in her forested front yard. Long enough for the sun to go down. Long enough for it to be creepy. Finally, when I felt like I couldn't put it off any longer, I cast a quick glance behind me and started walking home.

The curtains twitched in her window. A pair of hazel eyes vanished from sight.

My uncle's car had vanished from the driveway, but another had taken its place. One that was almost as familiar as my own. One that had no place being there tonight.

"Matt?"

He and my father were standing in the living room when I came inside. Foreheads bent together. Deep in a quiet discussion. They sprang apart when they saw me. Rather Matt took several quick steps back, while my father lifted his head fixing me in a steady gaze.

I stared between them in confusion. "I didn't know you were coming over."

Had I missed something? Something big? Matt *hated* my father. With the force of a tidal wave.

He'd hated him ever since the sixth grade when I'd showed up at his house covered in bruises. He'd hated him even more fiercely when I was punished with a hairline fracture and a black eye for breaking curfew. If it wasn't for the fact that my father was one of the most feared men on the planet, there's a chance Matt would take a swing at him.

So what were they doing conspiring in the living room?

"Why don't you boys run along upstairs?" my father suggested lightly. He reached into his pocket, pulling out a phone. "I'll call in some takeout for dinner."

I lingered there for a second, frozen with an inexplicable sense of dread, but Matt grabbed my arm and started jogging us up the stairs. "Sure. Thanks, Mr. Hunt."

"Good talking to you, Matt."

The two locked eyes for a split second before we disappeared into my room.

"What was *that*?" I demanded, yanking my arm free the second the door swung shut. Of all the things I needed to be dealing with right now, Matt Harris striking an inexplicable alliance with my father was *not* one of them.

He hesitated only a moment, and then pulled in a deep breath. "I told your dad...about Gabrielle."

For a second, I simply froze. Too stunned to speak. Too utterly overwhelmed by what was happening to take in his not-so-subtle implication. Then I took a jerking step back.

"...what about her?"

A distant part of me noted it was the first time he'd used her first name. Another part of me was spinning. We locked eyes for a moment, then he slowly shook his head.

"Don't make me say it. You know what."

My head jerked to the side. I was unable to speak.

"You remember that house party our freshman year, the one where Gabrielle..." He trailed off, forcing himself to meet my eyes. "Well, you didn't see the bathroom afterwards, but I did. Giant scorch marks all over the wall. The girl's one of them. I've known it for years."

I stared in horror, rooted to the spot. I'd been downstairs at the party in question, but I always remembered hearing Gabrielle's screams. We'd all just assumed she'd had too much to drink. Maybe mixed it with some pill combination her body couldn't tolerate. I'd never imagined it could be something else. That it could possibly be a horrifically timed supernatural awakening.

"Then why...?" I shook my head, too stunned to speak. "If you've known all this time, then why—"

"Because she decided to get involved with my best friend!" he shouted.

The words echoed between us, and I stared at him in shock.

"I've seen the way you guys look at each other," he continued passionately. "Don't even try to deny it, Jamie—you're a terrible liar. You were falling for her. I couldn't let that happen!"

He was already using the past tense. Like the house next door had already gone dark. My father's voice filtered up the stairs and my blood ran cold.

"Matt—"

"You of all people have to know why you can't be a part of something like that," he interrupted desperately. "I was trying to protect you!"

"Matty...you don't understand." I shook my head slowly, backing away from him. "You don't understand what they'll do to her."

Why I was pleading with him, I didn't know. At this point it just felt like I should be pleading with somebody, and there was no one left.

"She'll just disappear. We'll never see her again."

He stared at me for a second, then nodded his head. "Yeah. That's the plan."

Holy crap.

I was shaking from head to toe. In my mind, she was already in the back of a van. Every second I stood there was a second she didn't have. Every second I waited, the memory of her slipped farther away.

"Look," Matt started, softening his voice, placing a tentative hand on my shoulder. "I'm sorry, I actually am—but I didn't have a choice. It's done, Jamie. You need to let it go."

Hazel eyes flashed through my mind. A dusting of confetti drifting across her cheeks.

"Yeah...I'm sorry, too."

I knocked him down with a single punch. He wasn't expecting it. He didn't even have time to raise his hands. Just one hit and he fell back onto my bed. Eyes closed. Bleeding.

'Bye, Matty.

I didn't think. The time for thinking had passed. I didn't hesitate either. Hesitation would only get me killed. The second his head hit the pillow I was throwing open my window, leaping out into the open air before racing across the grass to the house next door.

I couldn't knock on the door—there was no door. I couldn't risk moving the table—there was a chance that my father would hear the noise. Instead, I climbed up to the second story and eased around the roof until I was standing outside her bedroom window.

She was sitting at her vanity, running a brush through her hair.

"Gabby!"

The brush clattered to the floor and she let out a shriek when she saw me. A shriek I could only hope wouldn't carry next door. In a flash she was on her feet, pulling open the glass.

"What the—? What're you doing here!" she demanded, clutching her chest in fright. "And why do you keep climbing up onto my—"

"They know about you," I interrupted. "They know you have the gene."

I wished there was an easier way to say it, but there wasn't time to waste. I'd seen how fast these people could mobilize. And my own father was the one mobilizing them.

She stepped away from the window, her lovely face turning pale.

"How do you know that?" she asked in a faltering voice. "I mean, how do you know for sure? Maybe it—"

I leapt inside, grabbing her hand in the same instant. "There's no time. You need to pack a bag and leave. You can't be here when they come." There was a brief pause. A pause during which my entire world changed "...we *both* need to leave. I can't be here either."

It was this more than anything that seemed to convince her. Not the fact that I was pale, or terrified, or I'd just jumped inside from the roof. But the fact that I'd decided to go.

She stared at me just a split second more, and then dove into her closet. When she emerged a second later, there was a giant backpack in her hand.

"I packed this almost a year ago," she murmured. "I just never knew..."

"I don't have anything," I blurted, suddenly anxious to get out all the facts. If she was looking for some kind of rescue—this wasn't it. "And I have no idea how to get out of here."

Maybe we shouldn't even go together. Maybe it would be better if we split up.

"It's okay," she murmured, taking my hand. "Leave that part to me."

Without another word, she dragged me down the stairs—pausing only to grab a thick wad of cash from the wooden chest near the door before doubling back down the hall to the back yard. I followed along silently, staring with wide eyes as she pulled back a tarp to reveal a beat-up car.

"My parents left this for me," she panted, tossing the backpack onto the seat. "It was their one condition if I was going to stay. They never thought I'd be safe here."

She leapt into the driver's seat, but I was rooted to the spot. Hadn't I just been down this road? Hadn't it ended in an Arizona jail?

"What about the plates?" I stalled for time, biting the inside of my cheek. "Won't they be able to track the plates—"

"It's not registered under my name," she hissed. "That's the point. Now get in!"

My eyes flickered next door. The lights were still on in my house. Matt was probably still unconscious on the bed. It would only be a matter of time before he woke. Before he let out a cry and alerted my father downstairs. Before a line was crossed and there was no turning back.

You crossed that line already. It's time to get in the car.

"Jamie—"

But I was already sliding in next to her, slumping low in the seat, peering out the tinted windows as we eased out the back of her property and slipped onto a main road. I twisted around as we streaked beneath the streetlamps, watching until my house disappeared from sight.

I imagined I could see it long after. A shadowy imprint burned into my mind.

"They're never going to stop following us."

It wasn't said as a question. I wasn't even sure I'd said it aloud. It was more of a passing thought. That fact was as certain as it was utterly terrifying.

Gabrielle sighed, keeping her eyes on the road. "No, I don't imagine they will."

We were quiet for a moment, and then she slipped her hand into mine. Our fingers laced together as we shut one door forever.

And opened another.

THE END

Illusion of Power

YOUR CURSE IS YOUR biggest strength.

I JUST DIDN'T KNOW it yet.

When Jamie and Gabrielle ran away in the middle of the night, they thought they'd be leaving their troubles behind them. Now, they're starting to realize those troubles have just begun.

With no money, no plan, and no destination, they find themselves the world's most wanted fugitives—trying to stay one step ahead of an international intelligence organization tasked with hunting them down. An intelligence organization run by Jamie's own father.

An opportunity presents itself, but nothing is as it seems. Alliances are strained. Powers are tested. And no one knows who to trust.

How do you outrun your destiny?

NEVER GIVE UP. NEVER give in.

Mending Magic Series

Lost Souls – Book 1
Illusion of Power – Book 2
Challenging the Dark – Book 3
Castle of Power – Book 4
Limits of Magic – Book 5
Protectors of Light – Book 6

Find W.J. May

Website:
http://www.wjmaybooks.com
Facebook:
https://www.facebook.com/pages/Author-WJ-May-FAN-PAGE/
141170442608149
Newsletter:
SIGN UP FOR W.J. May's Newsletter to find out about new releases, updates, cover reveals and even freebies!
http://eepurl.com/97aYf

More books by W.J. May

The Chronicles of Kerrigan

BOOK I - *Rae of Hope* **is FREE!**
  Book Trailer:
  http://www.youtube.com/watch?v=gILAwXxx8MU
  Book II - *Dark Nebula*
  Book Trailer:
  http://www.youtube.com/watch?v=Ca24STi_bFM
  Book III - *House of Cards*
  Book IV - *Royal Tea*
  Book V - *Under Fire*
  Book VI - *End in Sight*
  Book VII – *Hidden Darkness*
  Book VIII – *Twisted Together*
  Book IX – *Mark of Fate*
  Book X – *Strength & Power*
  Book XI – *Last One Standing*
  BOOK XII – *Rae of Light*

PREQUEL –
Christmas Before the Magic
Question the Darkness
Into the Darkness
Fight the Darkness
Alone the Darkness
Lost the Darkness

SEQUEL –
Matter of Time
Time Piece
Second Chance

Glitch in Time
Our Time
Precious Time

WHEN THE KING IS MURDERED, his only daughter, Katerina, must flee for her life. She finds herself on a strange and dangerous path. Alone for the first time she's forced to rely on her wits and the kindness of strangers, while protecting her secret at the same time.

Because she alone knows the truth. It was her brother who killed the king. And he's coming for her next.

Alone and struggling she finds herself an instant target, until a mysterious protector comes to her aid. Together, and with a collection of the most unlikely friends, the group must navigate through an enchanted world just as fantastical as it can be deadly. But time is not on their side.

With her brother's hired assassins closing in at every turn, Katerina must unlock a secret that's hidden deep inside her. It's the only thing strong enough to keep the darkness at bay.

Can she find the answers she needs? Will she ever take her rightful place on the throne?

Only one thing is certain...she's running out of time.

Hidden Secrets Saga:
Download Seventh Mark part 1 For FREE
Book Trailer:
http://www.youtube.com/watch?v=Y-_vVYC1gvo

Like most teenagers, Rouge is trying to figure out who she is and what she wants to be. With little knowledge about her past, she has questions but has never tried to find the answers. Everything changes when she befriends a strangely intoxicating family. Siblings Grace and Michael, appear to have secrets which seem connected to Rouge. Her hunch is confirmed when a horrible incident occurs at an outdoor party. Rouge may be the only one who can find the answer.

An ancient journal, a Sioghra necklace and a special mark force life-altering decisions for a girl who grew up unprepared to fight for her life or others.

All secrets have a cost and Rouge's determination to find the truth can only lead to trouble...or something even more sinister.

RADIUM HALOS - THE SENSELESS SERIES
Book 1 is FREE

Everyone needs to be a hero at one point in their life.

The small town of Elliot Lake will never be the same again.

Caught in a sudden thunderstorm, Zoe, a high school senior from Elliot Lake, and five of her friends take shelter in an abandoned uranium mine. Over the next few days, Zoe's hearing sharpens drastically, beyond what any normal human being can detect. She tells her friends, only to learn that four others have an increased sense as well. Only Kieran, the new boy from Scotland, isn't affected.

Fashioning themselves into superheroes, the group tries to stop the strange occurrences happening in their little town. Muggings, break-ins, disappearances, and murder begin to hit too close to home. It leads the team to think someone knows about their secret - someone who wants them all dead.

An incredulous group of heroes. A traitor in the midst. Some dreams are written in blood.

Courage Runs Red
The Blood Red Series
Book 1 is FREE

WHAT IF COURAGE WAS your only option?

When Kallie lands a college interview with the city's new hot-shot police officer, she has no idea everything in her life is about to change. The detective is young, handsome and seems to have an unnatural ability to stop the increasing local crime rate. Detective Liam's particular interest in Kallie sends her heart and head stumbling over each other.

When a raging blood feud between vampires spills into her home, Kallie gets caught in the middle. Torn between love and family loyalty she must find the courage to fight what she fears the most and possibly risk everything, even if it means dying for those she loves.

Daughter of Darkness - Victoria
Only Death Could Stop Her Now
The Daughters of Darkness is a series of female heroines who may or
may not know each other, but all have the same father, Vlad Montour.
Victoria is a Hunter Vampire

Don't miss out!

Visit the website below and you can sign up to receive emails whenever W.J. May publishes a new book. There's no charge and no obligation.

https://books2read.com/r/B-A-SSF-HOYU

BOOKS 2 READ

Connecting independent readers to independent writers.

Did you love *Lost Souls*? Then you should read *Eternal* by W.J. May!

She will fight for what is hers.

When the king is murdered, Katerina, his only daughter, must flee for her life. She finds herself on a strange and dangerous path. Alone for the first time, she's forced to rely upon her wits and the kindness of strangers, while protecting her royal secret at the same time.

Because she alone knows the truth. It was her brother who killed the king. And he's coming for her next.

Alone and struggling, she finds herself an instant target until a mysterious protector comes to her aid. Together, and with a collection of the most unlikely friends, the group must navigate through an enchanted world just as fantastical as it can be deadly. But time is not on their side.

With her brother's assassins closing in at every turn, Katerina must unlock a secret that's hidden deep inside her. The only thing strong enough to keep the darkness at bay.

Can she find the answers she needs? Will she ever take her rightful place on the throne?

Only one thing is certain: she's running out of time.

Be careful who you trust. Even the devil was once an angel.

Queen's Alpha Series: Eternal

Everlasting

Unceasing

Evermore

Forever

Boundless

Prophecy

Protected

Foretelling

Revelation

Betrayal

Resolved

Read more at www.wjmaybooks.com.

Also by W.J. May

Bit-Lit Series
Lost Vampire
Cost of Blood
Price of Death

Blood Red Series
Courage Runs Red
The Night Watch
Marked by Courage
Forever Night
The Other Side of Fear

Daughters of Darkness: Victoria's Journey
Victoria
Huntress
Coveted (A Vampire & Paranormal Romance)
Twisted
Daughter of Darkness - Victoria - Box Set

Paranormal Huntress Series
Never Look Back
Coven Master
Alpha's Permission
Blood Bonding
Oracle of Nightmares
Shadows in the Night
Paranormal Huntress BOX SET #1-3

Prophecy Series
Only the Beginning
White Winter
Secrets of Destiny

The Chronicles of Kerrigan
Rae of Hope
Dark Nebula
House of Cards
Royal Tea
Under Fire
End in Sight
Hidden Darkness
Twisted Together
Mark of Fate
Strength & Power
Last One Standing
Rae of Light
The Chronicles of Kerrigan Box Set Books # 1 - 6

The Kerrigan Kids
School of Potential

The Queen's Alpha Series
Eternal
Everlasting
Unceasing
Evermore
Forever
Boundless
Prophecy
Protected
Foretelling
Revelation
Betrayal
Resolved

The Senseless Series
Radium Halos - Part 1
Radium Halos - Part 2
Nonsense
Perception

Standalone
Shadow of Doubt (Part 1 & 2)
Five Shades of Fantasy

Shadow of Doubt - Part 1
Shadow of Doubt - Part 2
Four and a Half Shades of Fantasy
Dream Fighter
What Creeps in the Night
Forest of the Forbidden
Arcane Forest: A Fantasy Anthology
The First Fantasy Box Set

Watch for more at www.wjmaybooks.com.

About the Author

About W.J. May

Welcome to USA TODAY BESTSELLING author W.J. May's Page! SIGN UP for W.J. May's Newsletter to find out about new releases, updates, cover reveals and even freebies! http://eepurl.com/97aYf

Website: http://www.wjmaybooks.com

Facebook: http://www.facebook.com/pages/Author-WJ-May-FAN-PAGE/141170442608149?ref=hl *Please feel free to connect with me and share your comments. I love connecting with my readers.* W.J. May grew up in the fruit belt of Ontario. Crazy-happy childhood, she always has had a vivid imagination and loads of energy. After her father passed away in 2008, from a six-year battle with cancer (which she still believes he won the fight against), she began to write again. A passion she'd loved for years, but realized life was too short to keep putting it off. She is a writer of Young Adult, Fantasy Fiction and where ever else her little muses take her.

Read more at www.wjmaybooks.com.

Made in the USA
Monee, IL
23 September 2020